The Stone Goddess

Other *First Person Fiction* titles:

Behind the Mountains
by Edwidge Danticat

Flight to Freedom
by Ana Veciana-Suarez

Finding My Hat
By John Son

The Stone Goddess

Minfong Ho

SCHOLASTIC INC.
New York   Toronto   London   Auckland   Sydney
Mexico City   New Delhi   Hong Kong   Buenos Aires

This book was originally published in hardcover by Orchard Books in 2003.

ISBN 0-439-38198-3

12 11 10 9 8 7 6 5 4 3 2 1   5 6 7 8 9 10/0

Printed in the U.S.A.   40

First Scholastic paperback printing, April 2005

For Mom Rajawongse Smansnid Svasti,
our beloved "Mrs. Vanit,"
who taught me to love the English language
and claim it as my own.

Part One

*W*e moved as one, the trees, the river, even the clouds in the sky were stirred by the same silent force that was moving us as we danced. It was as if all motion was guided by the same rhythm, so that we were all part of each other, inseparable yet distinct.

We had been dancing for hours, going through the strict steps that we practiced each day in the palace's airy dance pavilion. Fingers flexed far back, wrist circling continuously, back arched, shoulders straight, ankles bent, feet alternately flat on the floor or lifting — every movement had to be controlled, and in perfect unison with the other dancers. It was late in the afternoon, and I should have been tired. But just then, a gust of wind stirred the still hot air, and suddenly I felt it — this strong sense that everything that moved was moving with that same silent rhythm.

As I danced, I looked around me. In the distance the avenue of grand old trees in the palace garden — the rain trees and the jacarandas and the casuarinas — were dipping their branches and rustling in unison, stirred by the breeze. Above them a few wisps of gray clouds sailed across the blue sky, reflected on the glistening surface of the Mekong River flowing just outside the palace walls. And as they moved, so I moved, because in dance we were moved by the same rhythm that moves the whole world.

Teeda was lifting one slim arm up, and so I did too, trained as I had been for years to dance behind my sister, following her every gesture, trying to be as graceful and natural as she was in her movements.

Like a goddess she was, like the apsaras of old that we were supposed to be, her gestures so precise and graceful that one flowed naturally into another. It looked so effortless, these subtle dance movements, and yet I knew it took years of disciplined training to do properly.

I felt a firm hand behind my shoulder, straightening it. Without turning I knew it was the dance teacher. I let her realign my arms too, and tried to keep that precise stance locked in my mind, while she moved back to correct the dancer behind me.

Then the teacher clapped her hands sharply, twice, signaling the end of the training session. The group of some fifty girls relaxed and started to disperse. As the dance teacher passed by, she reached out and touched my shoulder, so lightly it was barely a pat, but for that instant, she was not my teacher but my mother again. I smiled, knowing that Mother had noticed how well I had danced just now.

We were the lucky ones, I thought, Teeda and I, to have our own mother as our dance teacher. Our lessons would continue even after we left the palace grounds. Mother made us rehearse at home too, deftly tapping or twisting our stances closer to perfection. At this rate, I knew that Teeda would soon realize her dream. Some moonlit evening, she would be sewn into shimmering brocades, and as the musicians played on their flutes and drums and bamboo xylophones, she would perform the part of an *apsara*, a celestial dancer, before a rapt audience.

Quietly now, we waited until the last dancers had filed out of the pavilion, and then Teeda, my mother, and

I slipped into our sandals and walked out down the steps into the garden, then through a side gate of the palace walls back into the outside world.

The street outside seemed even more crowded and bustling than usual. Cars, buses, trishaws, and bicycles churned past, as people hurried along the sidewalks, weaving their way around the baskets of fruits and flowers set out by the street vendors.

A basket of lotus blossoms caught my eye, their pale pink a reflection of the twilight sky.

"Let's buy some!" I said, tugging at my mother. "We need some as temple offerings for the New Year." I could sense my mother weakening. As flowers sacred to Buddhism, we had always been taught that because the lotus had its roots in the mud, grew through the murky water, and blossomed in the open air, each lotus was like the human spirit.

"And we could use them to practice our apsara dance movements with you at home," Teeda added.

Relenting, our mother selected the freshest bouquet of lotuses, and hurriedly paid for them.

"You didn't bargain," I said, surprised.

"I want to get home before dark!" she snapped.

The shadows were lengthening as we turned down

the little side street that led to our house. When we arrived at our wooden gate, I was surprised that it was latched. I jiggled it, but it wouldn't open.

"It's locked," my father said, appearing behind it with my little brother, Yann. They must have been waiting for us, I realized. He unlocked a padlock around the latch.

"Pa! You're home so early," Teeda said. "Is something wrong?" He ignored the question, and ushered us inside, before locking the gate again.

"And why the lock?" I asked.

"Hush!" Ma said. "Just to be safe, that's all!"

But I did not feel safe. That night, I heard the sound of bombs falling again. Closer they were, and clearer than I had ever heard them, all through the night and into the morning.

At dawn, I was startled by a loud crashing sound. Was it thunder, or bombs? I tried to rouse myself; Teeda had said we should roll under the bed for cover if the bombs dropped really close by. Should I do that now? The explosions continued, on and on, and I imagined our house blowing up, collapsing around me. I jerked awake, breathing hard.

It is an awful thing, to wake up in a cold sweat, terrified.

But it wasn't bombs, I realized, only the steady beating of the temple drum nearby, summoning the monks to morning prayer. Strange, how a sound I had woken to every morning for as far back as I could remember, could now confuse and scare me. The drumming died down, and in the cool quiet of dawn, the hum of cicadas started up. It was the beginning of the hot season, and the cicadas had been hatching in the huge tamarind tree outside my window.

Ma came in through the bedroom doorway, her footsteps so light that Teeda, still sleeping in the bed next to mine, didn't stir at all.

Lifting aside the mosquito netting around my bed, Ma reached in and shook me gently. "Get up," she whispered, "if you want to see Boran."

Boran! My brother had just recently been ordained as a novice monk at the temple, and would be walking barefoot down our street with the other monks, ready to accept our offerings of food this morning. I had not seen him for weeks. Quickly, I got out of bed, and followed my mother downstairs.

In the kitchen she bustled about slicing vegetables, her cleaver deft and rhythmic against the wooden chopping board. I helped her ladle out fresh-steamed rice onto squares of banana leaves, as she folded the leaves into neat little pyramids.

"Let me!" I said.

Ma smiled, and handed me some toothpicks, which I used to skewer shut the tips of the pyramid shapes, so they would keep intact. She had tried to teach me how to make the shapes, but my fingers were too clumsy. Still, I liked poking the toothpicks through the folds of banana leaf.

"They're so light," I said, holding one up and weighing it in the palm of my hand. "Boran's going to be hungry."

My mother sighed. "Rice is getting harder to come by," she said quietly. "You know that, Nakri." I nodded. I had listened intently to the talk around the dinner table, because the grown-ups had sounded so serious and worried, but I hadn't absorbed much of it. My father had gotten angry about how corrupt the present Lon Nol government was getting; my mother had fretted about how the Communists were growing stronger, but I didn't feel that any of it really affected me.

Even if rice was harder to come by, Boran shouldn't have to go hungry, I thought. I would just slip two of these rice packets to him.

I helped my mother arrange the food packets on a round tray, and followed her out into the little street behind our house. Our neighbors were already there, waiting reverently for the procession of monks to accept their offerings.

It was just barely light when the monks turned down our lane, heads bowed and in single file. I stared at them, trying to make out which one was my brother. They all looked so much alike, with their heads shaved smooth and the orange robes fluttering slightly in the breeze. My mother tugged at my sleeve, which meant: *Stop staring!* Obediently I lowered my head. I had already caught a glimpse of Boran — he was the fifth one down the line.

Head bent, I could see only the line of bare feet approaching me. One by one, the bright orange cloths stopped at our small table of offerings, murmuring a blessing as my mother placed a packet of food in each bowl. When it was Boran's turn, I reached over and quickly put an extra rice packet into his bowl, and saw the smile that he wasn't quite quick enough to hide. Happy, I grinned back.

He was just about to move on, when from the opposite direction came a small convoy of jeeps, its tires churning up a cloud of dust on the dry road. Boran gasped and stumbled. As he did a packet of rice dropped to the ground by his bare feet.

Looking up, I saw dark, disheveled men dressed in black riding on top of the jeeps. Each one held an assault rifle at the ready. One of the men in the first jeep had a bullhorn, and was shouting through it.

"Surrender your weapons!" His voice boomed out in the early morning quiet. "The war is over! Raise a white flag and lay down your weapons at once!"

Mother had risen to her feet and was staring dumbfounded at the soldiers in their ragged black uniforms. Most of them had checkered scarves, worn and grimy with use, wrapped around their necks. They almost looked like farmers coming back from their rice fields.

"Already?" Ma whispered. "They've won?"

As if in answer to her question, the voice boomed out, "Comrades, victory is ours! We are the Angkar. We are the new government of Kampuchea!"

The convoy of jeeps swept past us in a swirl of dust, narrowly missing the line of silent monks.

My father came rushing out of the house and grabbed my mother's wrist, pulling her back into our garden. "Nakri, child! Come in quickly!" he shouted at me over his shoulder, his voice urgent.

I started running along with them, then stopped. The packet of rice Boran had dropped was still lying in the dust. Should I run back and pick it up? But my father was already pulling shut the wooden gates to our yard, and so I darted past him and slipped in before the gates were shut and locked.

Elsewhere in the city, we could hear the sound of car horns blaring and bicycle bells ringing. People were celebrating the end of the long civil war.

Along our street, neighbors were already flying white flags from their balconies and windows. "We don't have a white flag," I said.

"Make one," Pa answered. "Anything will do — a pillowcase, a shirt — just tie it to a bamboo pole and stick it out your window."

That sounded almost like a game. I called out to Yann, who was peeking down over the bannister, and together we went off to make a white flag, leaving our parents to listen to the radio.

"What will happen now?" I heard my mother asking.

"Who knows?" Pa said. "We'll just have to wait and see."

We didn't have to wait very long.

Later that morning, more of those ragged soldiers came by, this time on foot. They were all armed, but were so gaunt and tired that they looked more like beggars than victorious soldiers. Some were barefoot, others had on black sandals with soles cut from rubber tires, and straps of inner tubing. Many of them didn't look much older than my teenage brother, Boran. They came up to our gate, and held a brief, urgent conversation with Pa. When he walked back into our house, Pa was looking grim.

"They say we have to leave the city immediately. Americans are going to bomb it any minute. We should pack enough for three days, they said; then it will be safe to come back."

For some time now American planes had been carpet-bombing the surrounding countryside. Thousands of farmers had flooded into our city to take refuge from them. If they were going to bomb Phnom Penh now that it had fallen into Communist control, it seemed only logical that everyone inside the city should leave.

"What about Boran?" Mother was asking.

"He's coming home from the monastery. I've already told him to," Pa said. "You start packing."

My mother started to gather food and clothes and wrap them in tight bundles.

As we packed, I became aware of the silence. It was almost eerie. For the first time in months, there were no sounds of war in the distance, no muffled explosions of artillery shells, no crackle of gunfire, no scream of sirens. Instead, the cicadas and tree frogs took over, filling the silence of the night with their natural cadences. If this is what peace sounds like, I thought, I would have no trouble sleeping soundly.

And yet none of us slept well at all. I went to sleep at my usual bedtime, but during the night I woke up several times, aware that my parents were still up, talking in low voices, packing and repacking what would be taken. Once, I heard Ma crying, her sobs coming out soft and jagged. The sound of it bothered me more than the sounds of bombing and gunfire had.

In the morning, I sorted out a few of my most prized possessions too, preparing to pack them. In a pile on my bed were my new pencil box, a silk sarong, a silver belt, and my photo album.

When I showed my mother these things, she shook her head impatiently, and said I couldn't bring any of them.

"Why not? You and Pa are bringing so much," I protested. Even now, I could see my father strapping bulky packages of clothing and food onto the back of his motor scooter.

"Just do as I say," Ma snapped.

"But I want to take . . ." My lower lip was quivering.

"Listen, why don't you take the belt, that silver belt," Teeda broke in. "Look, Ma, she can even wear it under her blouse, like this." Teeda belted the chain of wrought silver around my waist. "And it might come in useful," she added softly.

"All right," my mother said. "But nothing else!" Abruptly she turned and left the room.

"Why is Ma so angry?" Yann whimpered, his big eyes brimming with tears. I could tell he was about to lose control and start crying.

"Don't cry — look what I have!" Teeda said. Quickly she rummaged in the top drawer of our bureau and brought out a thin book, the photo album that she had pasted our family photographs in. Carefully she placed it in Yann's hands. "Look," she said, flipping open to the first page. "There's you, as a baby. And here's one of all of us, on New Year's Day. You've got your new belt on. See how shiny the buckle is?"

Yann smiled. "I could pack that buckle," he said. "It's still shiny."

"You do that. I won't tell Ma, all right?" Teeda whispered, smiling at him.

Yann nodded, blinking away his tears.

"Now let's go down for some breakfast. I'll make us some noodles," Teeda said, scooping him up in her arms and leading the way down to the kitchen. I followed behind them, feeling comforted too.

We sat down at the kitchen table, and within minutes Teeda was sliding big bowls of noodles across the table to each of us. There were droplets of oil glistening on the surface of the soup, and bits of scallion and coriander floating on top. I took a sip of broth and savored it. It was delicious.

By late morning we were ready to go. Announcements had been made over loudspeakers that everyone who had relatives in the countryside should return to those villages and stay there until it was safe to return to Phnom Penh again. My parents had held discussions in low urgent voices about it, and decided that we should all go to Siem Reap, where Ma's parents still lived.

Boran had come home earlier that day, not in the saffron robes of the novice monk but in ordinary street clothes, although he still looked a little strange because of his shaved head.

As he helped my father strap the last of the bundles and boxes onto the scooter, I slipped back to my own room, thinking that I could retrieve my photo album and bring that along. I head my father yelling, "Nakri, we are leaving. NOW!"

I looked through the doorway into my room. A shaft of morning light filtered through the leaves of the mango tree outside, casting a pool of lacy shadows on the smooth wooden floor. Over in the far corner was my bed, still unmade, the gauzy mosquito netting lifting a little, stirred by a passing breeze. My photo album was under it, on the bed, next to my pillow, where I had tucked it away for safekeeping last night. I opened it, and an envelope fell out. It had a letter from America, sent by a colleague of my father's who had visited us the year before. There was a card in it, and a photograph taken of our whole family with the foreigner, standing in front of our house.

"Nakri! NOW!" my father yelled.

"And don't bring anything more with you," my mother added. I could tell they were both serious.

Quickly, I slipped the photo back into its envelope, and tucked it back inside the photo album. If I couldn't take it with me, I decided, at least I would hide it. I reached up on tiptoe to the top drawer of the dresser, where Teeda kept her crystal globe safely out of Yann's reach. Sure enough, there was the ball, back in its place. I tucked my photo album in beside it, and closed the drawer, promising myself that I would retrieve it the first chance I got.

Then I stood back and took one last look at the room, trying to imprint it in my mind as if it too was a photograph: the mango tree outside the screen window, the two twin beds, the two sequined dance costumes hanging side by side in the closet. It was a space I had shared all my life with my sister, and everything in it was so familiar that it had almost become part of me. Yet I could take nothing of it with me — except this one last image.

I shut my eyes tight, and tried to take in the image of my room as if I was a camera myself. Only then was I able to turn and walk away.

We left the house with food and clothes, pots and pans, mats and nets and medicine and documents and money and jewelry and photographs. The streets were choked with people like ourselves, laden down with things, pushing bicycles and motorcycles, wheelbarrows and carts, even cars and trucks, piled high with their belongings.

At every intersection there were those soldiers in

black, waving their guns at us to keep walking — always walking away from the city center and toward the outskirts. Our family tried hard to keep close together, and move as a unit, but it was hard because people were jammed up against us from every direction.

The main boulevard was even more crowded and chaotic. The convoys of jeeps were still cruising around, but there were cars jammed full of people and belongings clogging the road.

In the distance, rising above the swirl of the crowd, I saw the tall, sloping roof of the palace, its orange tiles gleaming in the sun. Below it was the smaller roof of the dance pavilion, its upward curve a visual echo of the palace. It seemed incredible that I had been dancing in tranquil silence under it, just two days ago.

Through the rest of that long afternoon, we kept walking, although the roads were so jammed that we did not make much headway at all. It was like being caught up in a monsoon drain, moving with the sludge and leaves and debris slowly but surely in one direction. At the major street corners would be groups of those armed soldiers in black, making sure that we all moved only one way — out of the city.

By the side of the road, there were piles of belongings

discarded by people who had found themselves too heavily laden down. Piles of clothes, a few radios, even a sewing machine had been abandoned. At first Ma poked through some of the piles, probably hoping to scavenge something, but after a while she didn't seem interested or curious anymore.

We were having trouble just keeping all our belongings with us. Yann had gotten tired of walking, and so Pa let him perch on the handlebars of the scooter. I tried to keep holding onto the bundle entrusted to me, but my feet started hurting. A blister was forming on the big toe of my left foot, and with every step my rubber sandals rubbed against it. I started whimpering and Teeda took my bundle for me, but I could see she was getting tired too.

By nightfall we had reached only the outskirts of the city. People were stopping and setting up temporary little campsites anywhere they could, under a tree, against a stone wall, or just in some patch of open space. Little campfires flickered in the dusk.

Pa decided to stop next to a hibiscus hedge, its flowers a deep crimson even under a coat of dust. We spread out our sleeping mats, and Ma unwrapped a woven basket of cooked rice that she had prepared. There were some hard-boiled eggs, garnished with bits of fried garlic, and we sat in a semicircle, and started our meal.

Nearby, a family, which must have arrived earlier, had set up a charcoal stove, and was roasting strips of chicken skewered onto long sticks. The smell of the meat was mouthwatering. Ma approached them, and asked if she could buy a few strips. I saw the other woman nod, and soon some roast meat and money were changing hands.

Suddenly, a soldier in black appeared out of the gloom, his rifle pointing up, and demanded to know what was going on. Before Ma could explain, he had snatched the money from her hands, and thrown the bills into the fire.

"No more buying and selling!" he shouted. "The Angkar has forbidden it. This is the New Society. The Angkar will provide for all your needs!" He kicked sand over the fire, smothering not only the fire but all the bits of roast meat as well.

It was the first time I had heard the word "Angkar" used like this. The word just meant "group" or "organization" — but he was invoking it as if it were the name of some mighty king. Did he mean the Khmer Rouge, the Communists that Father spoke of with such hushed dread? What is so great about this Angkar, I wanted to ask, if it provides for us by kicking dirt onto our food? But I only watched in silence as the other woman picked out the scraps of chicken and tried to shake the sand loose from them. Already I was learning not to ask questions.

It took us over ten days of walking before we reached the outskirts of Phum Spean Tnaot village in Siem Reap province, still twenty miles from where my grandparents lived. By then we were all so tired that we were walking very slowly, even though the crowds had thinned out quite a bit. Along the way several "Registration Centers" had been set up, where a few cadres would sit behind a long table as whole families stood before them, answering their questions as they jotted down answers on sheets of paper. We had resisted being "registered" because Pa felt it was better just to get to our grandparents' village first.

Yann had grown so tired and limp that he had to be carried. It was decided that Pa would leave us and our belongings under a tree, and ride his scooter the rest of the way into Phum Spean Tnaot. Maybe, they thought, my grandfather could come out with an oxcart to meet us.

We unloaded all the bundles and packages from the scooter, and Pa climbed onto the seat. As he kick-started the engine to life, I wanted to call out to him for permission to go along. Instead, I stood by in silence. That familiar impulse — to tag along, to tease my parents for special favors — seemed already to belong to a bygone age, to a much younger me.

But my father surprised me. Twisting back on his seat, he looked at me and asked if I wanted to ride behind him. My heart leapt. There was nothing I loved more than to ride behind him on his scooter. Eagerly, I climbed up onto the seat behind him, and wrapped my arms tightly around his waist. I felt rather than heard his laugh, as the scooter puttered to a slow start, then picked up speed.

I pressed my cheek against his back, feeling the familiar ridge of his spine under his shirt, as the wind streamed against my hair and my bare arms. Such a thrill it always was to feel both the excitement of speed and the safety of being with my father at the same time!

"Nicer than walking, eh, little one?" my father said, calling me by my pet name, something he hadn't done for some time. His face was turned back, and I could just see the edge of his smile. To answer I just hugged him harder.

Within an hour we arrived at my grandparents' house. I knew we were there by the rhythmic *click-click*ing of my grandmother's loom. Whenever we visited, for as far back as I could remember, she would be seated at the wooden bench under the stilts of her house, weaving at the loom. From one side to the other, her shuttle would zip across and between the meshed tiers of threads, back and forth, back and forth.

Sure enough, she was at it now. Without missing a beat, her hands still deftly sliding the shuttle back and forth, she looked up at us and smiled.

For a moment I felt as if nothing had changed, that we were just on one of our family visits here for the school holidays. It wasn't that time had stopped, but more that it had simply taken on the little back-and-forth movement of the shuttle in her loom. Then I noticed the cloth she was weaving, and understood that the cadres, with their severe idea of Angkar, must have already taken over the village. Instead of the usual colorful checkered patterns of reds, oranges, and yellows, every thread on her loom was black.

At first the changes were so small that we could almost pretend nothing much had really changed. Yes, the threads on Grandma's loom were all black, and even all the once-colorful shirts and blouses, the checkered scarves and patterned sarongs that villagers wore, had been boiled in vegetable dyes until they turned black. But such changes seemed only minor at first. Our grandparents were still warm and welcoming, and their house was just as I had remembered it from past school holidays.

We moved in with them, and although they didn't have a big house, it was clean and airy — with broad teak floor planks, and a thick palmetto thatch roof, which kept it cool in the midday sun and dry in the monsoon rains. There was a little orchard of fruit trees they had in the backyard, and I taught Yann how to climb onto their branches to pick ripe star fruits and mangoes and rambutans.

The best part was, I had Teeda all to myself. Without her schoolmates and friends around, she became resigned to spending her time with me. Considering that at seventeen, she was almost five years older than me, this was an honor that I wouldn't even have dreamed of back in the city.

Teeda was determined to keep practicing her dance steps. At first she would go through them alone, like she did at home, leaving me to imitate her as best I could. But when it became apparent that Ma wasn't going to train either of us anymore ("It's dangerous," Ma scolded. "People might notice, and disapprove"), Teeda started to help me with my movements.

She helped me practice making the seven basic hand gestures used throughout Cambodian classical dance: how to cup my hands so that my fingers would look like a flower blossoming, or how to point, by extending the index finger while the others are rounded to touch the thumb. Harder were the two gestures of the *lear* and *cheap*, often used in pairs to symbolize "leaf and flower," or "question and answer," or "man and woman." To do that, Teeda would arch my fingers back as far as they would go, while bending my thumb to my palm, or else joining my thumb with my index finger. Although I tried to do the same hand-flexing exercises as Teeda did, I couldn't make my fingers bend as far back as she could. "Keep trying," she would say. "You've just got to keep at it." And I would, because I wanted to be like her.

I also learned to play simple melodies on a reed flute that my grandfather had made, and which he taught me to play. Sometimes I would play as Teeda danced, pretending that I was the whole orchestra that would have accompanied her if she was performing in the palace.

But what I loved most was when she performed the entire sequence of dance steps in her role as an apsara, a dancing goddess. And not just any apsara, but the white apsara — the central figure in the dance of these graceful goddesses. Dressed all in shimmering white, with an elaborate headdress of gold, she would lead the other apsaras in a slow, supple dance originally meant for only the gods. Teeda had been training for the role for years during those long afternoons of dancing in the palace pavilion. It was a great honor to have been designated to dance that role, and Teeda had never performed it before an audience, although it had always been her dream to.

And I would dance behind her, as one of the lesser apsaras, mimicking her in every arch of her fingers, every lift of the ankle, every thrust of the shoulder.

And so, much like we did at home, we would quietly practice our dance segments every morning, in a corner of our grandmother's old teak house. And my little world felt secure and intact.

And yet, as the weeks passed, it was hard to pretend that this was just another one of those school holidays that we used to spend in the village.

The grown-ups held whispered conversations deep into the night, when they thought Yann and I had gone to sleep. By the flickering light of the kerosene lamp, I would see their shadows loom on the walls. One night, I saw my father take out the documents he had brought with him — all our birth certificates and property deeds and his graduation diploma — and look at them for a long time, his glasses glinting in the dim light. Then he slipped them into a plastic bag and carefully tucked it under the thatched roofing in the eaves.

There was a silent watchfulness in the village that I had never known before. Neighbors watched each other, but pretended not to. We were among the first of the new arrivals in the village, but instead of the usual cheerful greetings from old friends and neighbors of my grandparents, there was only this sense of suspicion, as if we were all strangers and knew better than to trust each other. When other people trickled in from the city, tired and laden with all their belongings, we didn't help or acknowledge them, either, but only sat in the shadows and watched.

I noticed that the same kind of black-uniformed soldiers that had lined the main roads, directing us away from the city, were also to be found in the village, prowling around in tight groups of twos or threes, often armed. They watched us, and we watched them.

Then, as if at some invisible signal, they acted. One morning they marched through the village, and announced that there would be a big meeting of the whole village — both new arrivals and the original villagers — at the temple courtyard that afternoon. Everyone, they said, was invited to attend.

"Invited?" my father grunted. "Ordered, he means."

"Hush!" Ma said, frowning. "You talk too much."

"She's right, Hoon," my grandfather spoke up, unexpectedly. "Even the walls have ears now." It was unusual for Grandpa to rebuke my father, especially in front of us children. Always in the past, the old man had treated his son-in-law with respect, even deference, because my father was educated, and a teacher, and had a job in the city. Whenever there was a discussion, my father would hold forth, giving his opinion, as Grandpa sat and listened, nodding. Now my father was the one who sat in silence, tight-lipped, as the old farmer told him to be careful, to admit nothing, to keep quiet. "One more thing, Hoon," Grandpa said. "I think you should take off your glasses, and hide them."

"What? Why should I?" my father asked.

"You know why," Grandpa said. "They do not trust city people, especially educated ones."

"But . . . how will I see clearly? How can I read anything?"

"You won't," the old man said simply. He held out his hands for the glasses. "Please," he said. "It's better this way."

Reluctantly, my father took off his horn-rimmed glasses and handed them over. His face looked bare and vulnerable without them.

Grandpa took the pair of glasses and put them carefully into the hollow of a piece of bamboo. Without a word, he buried the bamboo in some loose dirt underneath Grandma's loom. "They will be there, waiting for you, when all this is over," he said.

My father did not answer. He rubbed his eyes, and when he looked up, there was a blank, lost look to them.

Pa took my hand when we walked over to the temple for the meeting later that afternoon, so that I could guide him. He had been nearsighted for so long that he didn't trust himself without his glasses.

Hand in hand, we stepped over the raised doorjamb of the temple door, and entered into the courtyard enclosed by old whitewashed walls. It was quiet there, with only the first few villagers starting to arrive. Silently we looked around. In the sandy courtyard, shaded by the heart-shaped leaves of huge Po trees, was the sanctuary of the main temple. There, a stately Buddha image stood, one hand raised in his timeless gesture of calming all enemies. Automatically, I put my palms together and bowed to the statue, in the gesture of respect I had been taught to do since I was a child. To my surprise, however, Pa did not do the same thing.

As we approached the sanctuary, I saw someone step out of the shadows and lift up a hoe, aiming it right at the Buddha statue. With one blow, he had smashed in the statue's face.

I gasped.

"What is it?" Pa whispered.

The words stuck in my throat. There was no way to describe what I was seeing. I could not say anything. In the silence, the only sound was the thud of the metal hoe head against stone as the man in black kept smashing the statue. In the distance was the quiet tinkling of the temple bells on the eaves high above us.

Then, with a final whack, the soldier knocked off the upheld palm of the statue. It fell with a heavy thud onto the ground, and stayed there, motionless.

Ignoring us, the soldier tossed aside his hoe, and walked off briskly.

My father let go of my hand, and slowly made his way over to the statue. Its face was badly dented, its once-smooth cheeks and elegant smile now a web of jagged little craters. Pa reached up and touched it, his fingers exploring the battered stone surface. Often as a child I had watched him gently rub thin pieces of gold leaf onto this statue, in the age-old custom of reverence, as we prayed to the Buddha. Now, I saw only how his fingers fumbled at the scarred surface of the statue's shoulder, then down along its arm, until finally they stopped at the truncated wrist. For a long moment, Father's fingers groped at the empty air, searching for the stone hand that wasn't there anymore.

"Pa, let's go," I said, tugging at my father.

Other villagers were coming in now. Behind me I heard gasps, shocked whispers as they too saw the mutilated Buddha.

I reached out for Father's fumbling fingers, and

pulled them away from the statue. As we walked away, I could feel his hand trembling in mine.

Nothing that the soldiers said that afternoon made any sense to me. Their words were as incomprehensible as the ancient Pali chants I used to hear the monks intoning at temple festivals. The difference was that the monks were quiet and still, with calming and melodious voices. These soldiers yelled.

Harsh words, they were too, infused with hatred and anger. "Revolution! Sacrifice!" "Armed Struggle." "Communism-imperialism-capitalism. . . ." And running like a thick thread through it all was always that same word: "Angkar!"

Every so often, the main speaker, a slightly pudgy man with close-cropped graying hair, would punctuate his speech with a raised fist and some slogan like "Long Live the Revolution!" And we were all expected to get to our feet, raise our fists, and shout, "Long live the Revolution!" Father resisted getting up at first, but he couldn't see the armed soldiers patrolling the wall of the courtyard, their rifles pointed casually at us. I saw them, and so, grimly, I would pull Pa to his feet, and shout doubly loud, to make up for his silence.

At the end of the meeting, the cadres sang the new national anthem:

"We love the Angkar . . .
The Angkar brings us health and strength.
We live in the commune,
Where the light of the Revolution shines on us.
Oh Angkar, we love you so deeply
That we resolve to follow the glorious red path you
    lay before us!"

In double file the cadres danced and sang about the glory of the Angkar — the Organization, the Communist Party, the Khmer Rouge leadership. It had been explained to us what this all-powerful, all-pervasive Angkar was, but in my mind I thought of it as a huge spider hovering over us, spinning its web over our lives and our land, its long legs reaching out to control our every movement.

That night, after the meeting was finally over, I heard Pa talking softly to Boran and the others. "We have no place in this New Society they keep talking about," he said. "They want to force Cambodia into being a country of peasants and soldiers, completely closed off from the world. Anybody else, teachers and doctors and business owners and artists, they despise and are afraid of."

My grandfather nodded. "And that's why you, Hoon, have to speak carefully."

He did try, Pa did. I heard him, several days later, when three Khmer Rouge soldiers came to the house, and asked to talk to him. My grandmother was weaving at her loom, and so I slipped downstairs and sat down on the wooden bench next to her. At the opposite corner of the house, under the tall stilts, was a low platform of split bamboo, and this was where my father gestured for the soldiers to sit down.

Although their voices were low, I could still make out what they were saying between the rhythmic clicks of the shuttle. I knew that Grandma too was listening intently, although her hands kept busy with the threads.

"Where did you live, before you came here?" one of the cadres asked him.

"In Phnom Penh, on Street 336 behind the Dang Kor Market," my father said, naming a poor section on the southwest edge of the city.

"What did you do?"

"I repaired bicycles. And motorcycles, scooters. I

worked in a small bicycle shop that belonged to someone called Nem Yin."

"Were you ever part of counterrevolutionary Lon Nol's army?"

My father shook his head.

"Or the police force? Or a bureaucrat in the lackey government?"

"No, comrade, never," my father said, using the term that they all used for us, for each other.

"Did you go to high school? University? Can you read and write foreign languages?"

Pa squinted at them with his nearsighted eyes. "Would I be changing bicycle tires all day if I could?" he asked.

"Just answer the question!"

"No," Pa said.

On and on the questioning went, many of them repeated several times. But my father was careful, and never wavered or varied his answers.

Yet still they were not satisfied. As they got up to leave, one of them pointed to our old scooter, leaning against the wall, and said, "That tire looks a bit flat. Why don't you check it?"

"Check it?" Pa echoed, a tinge of uncertainty in his

voice. "You mean take out the inner tube to check for punctures?"

The cadre nodded. "Go ahead," he said.

My father took a deep breath, and walked over to his scooter. Normally, he could have done it deftly enough, since he was quite good at fixing things. But without his glasses, and perhaps because he was nervous, his hands were clumsy as he tried to unscrew the little cap to the air valve.

The soldiers watched him skeptically.

"My fingers are stiff," Pa said, looking up at them as he knelt by the scooter. "I . . . I sprained my wrist last week . . ."

"I see," the cadre said, then added, "Comrade . . ."

They exchanged a meaningful look and then, without another word, turned and walked away.

When they returned two days later, it was with an ox-cart. Five other men were already in the cart, looking subdued and a little scared. It had all been arranged. Father was to go with them, to be taken off to a "re-education camp" somewhere in the forest, where he would join a group of other men to learn how to be a leader in the New Society. It was an honor to be chosen, they had said, and Father would learn some important new things.

"An honor it might be," Pa had said softly to us the night before, "but a choice it is not."

My mother had started to weep quietly, but he had patted her and said, "A month — that's how long they said it will take. I'll be back in a month. Everything will be fine."

But my mother had only continued to weep.

Her tears scared me, and so I started to cry too. Father held my head gently, cupping my ears in his big hands, and told me to be strong, and help take care of the family. "Keep watch on that moon too," he said, pointing to the crescent moon rising through the palm fronds outside the window. "Watch it with me. We'll each watch it grow full, and then wane. And when it's shaped like that again, I will be back," he said.

And so, after he had gone, I kept watch on the moon, imagining each night that he was watching it too, and thinking of us. On cloudy nights I lay on my mat, and watched it sail through the silver-rimmed clouds. On clear nights I watched it rise up above the horizon until it was tangled in the palm trees, and I would fall asleep.

On rainy nights — of which there were more and more because the monsoons were starting — I couldn't see it at all, and had to be satisfied just thinking about it. I watched it grow round, and then shrink down to nothing. When finally it started growing again, I watched eagerly as it started to assume the crescent shape it had been when Pa had left.

There it hung, the crescent moon, for three nights, before it became too rounded to be considered a crescent anymore. And still he did not come.

I knew I was not supposed to ask questions, but I couldn't help it. I asked my mother when Pa was coming back, but she only turned away without replying. I asked Boran, and Teeda, and my grandfather, but they also remained silent. And by the time the moon was full again, I did not ask anymore.

The silence had a weight to it. It weighed me down just as surely as a slab of stone laid on my chest would weigh me down. I stopped asking about Pa, and the others stopped talking about him. Yet we still waited, and I still watched the moon. But always in this heavy silence.

The rains were coming more often now, and by the time the moon was full again, it had become our turn to leave the village. It was time for the rice seedlings to be transplanted, the "comrades" told us. Our help was needed in villages to the southwest. A big truck would come to take away all of us "new people," about thirty urban families who had come into the village after the liberation of Cambodia. We would be relocated to another province, over sixty miles away. There, we were told, we would have newly built houses waiting for us, and rice fields already ploughed and harrowed, ready for new seedlings. But because Yann was so young, they allowed Ma to stay in her village in Siem Reap with him. Only Boran, Teeda, and I would have to leave.

Did we believe them? We had been told that we'd be returning home in three days, when we were being forced to evacuate Phnom Penh. Then we had been told that Father would return in a month, after they took him away. Now we were being told we were going to more prosperous villages with fields fertile enough to yield plenty of rice for us. Should we believe them now, when they had lied to us twice before?

My older brother and sister, even my mother, didn't seem to question them. Or if they did, it was never done out loud. Perhaps from the very beginning, they realized that it would be no use to ask questions, because they could never hope to get a true answer. Or perhaps they thought: How would knowing the answers change anything anyway?

March, they said — and we marched. *Move*, they said — and we moved. *Sit. Listen. Work. Obey.* And we did. We did it knowing that if we didn't obey, we would be severely punished, perhaps killed. But we did it also because we clung to the ever more distant hope that things would get better, if only we could endure it just a bit longer.

As Buddhists, we accepted suffering. The old Buddhist monks had taught us that suffering was part of life, that as human beings we were all tied to the Wheel of Suffering, which kept revolving but which never changed its path.

Then the Communist cadres told us that heavy work was part of life, that we were tied to the Wheel of History. Either way, it was this great wheel that moved relentlessly, dragging us with it. We couldn't stop it, we couldn't get out of its way, we could only submit as it rolled, ever so slowly and surely, over us.

And so when we were told we had to move out of my grandparents' home, we made our preparations quietly. Much of the belongings we had brought from Phnom Penh four months ago had already been used up — the food supplies and soap and oil. Things like radios and cameras and motorbikes had become useless shells of themselves, ever since they had run out of batteries or film or gasoline. And other things, like watches and books and fancy clothes, had become simply irrelevant. So when we packed this time, we didn't take much with us at all — just a change of clothing and some sandals. My grandmother had finished weaving a simple *kraama* on her loom, and this she solemnly gave to Teeda to use as a shawl, or towel, or scarf. Rather than the bright colors and intricate designs that she used to weave, this piece of cloth was very plain — just black-and-white checkered — but Teeda accepted it with both hands, as if it were a precious gift.

The night before we were to leave, I slipped downstairs and dug out the bamboo with Pa's glasses inside. The bamboo casing had turned brown, but the glasses were still intact. I wiped them on my sarong, carefully wiping the lenses clean as Pa had done countless times before. Then I put them back, careful to put them in exactly the same shallow hole where they had been buried. When he comes back for them, I told myself, they would be polished clean for him.

Part Two

"Remember the garden . . . . coming in through the side gate of those thick walls to enter the garden, with the hibiscus and orchids and roses all in bloom. See the row of palm trees on your right, along the river, as you walk toward it. You can see the wide steps leading up to the pavilion. Walk up those steps, and onto the smooth tiles of the dance floor. Look at the columns holding up the roof, then look down at the tiles on the floor. What's the design on them? What colors are they?"

As my sister talked, so softly that only I heard her, I closed my eyes and followed her words, down the grassy path to the dance pavilion. I can feel the grass cool beneath my bare feet; I can see the dappled shadows of the palm fronds; I hear the laughter of the other dancers as they come up the steps to the pavilion. I walk up the steps myself, marveling at the vast space of the airy hall. It is all there still, just as we had left it that last day of rehearsal. And the tiles on the floor. I think back, searching my memory, and an image comes. "Dark brown squares set within beige ones, with a crisscross design at the margin," I said softly. "Cool and smooth and swept so clean that I can feel even a grain of sand underfoot."

"Nice," Teeda said.

I opened my eyes slightly, and saw that she was smiling at me. But her face had grown so gaunt that her smile looked slightly lopsided. She was lying on the scarf that Grandma had woven for us just before we left, its edges now frayed from use. A shaft of morning light filtered through a hole in the flimsy thatched roof above us, and fell on the dirt floor. Teeda's thin metal bowl and spoon hung on a nail nearby, the only possessions she had left.

I shut my eyes, and willed myself out of this awful place that we have lived in for so long, trying to imagine myself somewhere else.

"My turn," I said. In my mind I have entered the kitchen, and am standing in front of the stove. "Walk through the kitchen doorway," I said to Teeda, and I know that as she is lying beside me, her eyes are closed too. "There is a pot of rice cooking on the far left. The charcoal is glowing under it, and steam rises from the pot. Next to it is a pot of curry, chicken curry — and if you lift the lid you can see carrots and green peppers simmering in it."

"You always go to the kitchen," she sighed, but it was not a complaint. Where else would you want to go, after all, if you were hungry? And we were always hungry. In fact, I could hardly remember back to a time when we weren't hungry. I knew that in our "old" lives, before the Angkar, we would sit down at mealtimes at home, and eat until we were full — but it hardly seemed possible, or real, anymore.

How long ago had it been since Teeda, Boran, and I, together with about a hundred and twenty other newly arrived youngsters, were gathered from different areas and forced to relocate here, in Phum Thmei — "New Village"? It was new all right, so new that we had built most of it, cutting down saplings to stake out the posts of the flimsy huts that we were now sleeping in, and weaving together the palmetto thatching ourselves. We also helped build a smaller but sturdier house, higher off the ground, for the cadres who supervised us.

For over a year now, our lives had been confined to those huts, leaving them only to eat at the main dining hall, or to work out in the fields. If Teeda and I hadn't played our memory game, it would have been easy to believe that this was the entirety of our world, and that we had no life before it, or outside of it.

"The kitchen," I reminded her now. "Think of the big white refrigerator next to the sink. Imagine pulling it open, and feeling the rush of cold air come out at you. There is a freezer section on top. Open it — what is on the very bottom, on the right?"

Teeda frowned, trying to think. "Give me a hint," she said.

"It's long and metal, and always filled."

"The ice-cube tray," she whispered, awed at the sudden memory. "I can taste the ice now. It's so cold it numbs my tongue!"

"Save some for me," I said, happy that I have evoked such a pleasant memory for her. "Unless there's some Popsicles in there?"

Teeda remained silent. She was not playing anymore.

"It's time to get up," she said, and when I protested weakly, she became more insistent, shaking me by the shoulders gently. "You know we'll be punished if we're late again."

And so, reluctantly, I opened my eyes.

No matter how often I woke up to this scene, I still felt a sense of dismay at what I saw, so bleak compared with what I had been used to in my childhood. About forty other girls were all lying in a disheveled row down the side of this long, narrow shed, each of them as thin and tired as Teeda and I were.

Streaks of a pale dawn filtered through the walls of bamboo slats and the flimsy thatched roof. Some of the other girls were stirring, and already a few of them were struggling to get up. Teeda sat up, and tugged at me. She had grown so thin that her shoulder bone jutted out sharply under her black shirt. There was a hole in the middle of her left sleeve, and her elbow poked out of it at a bony angle. My beautiful sister, who once looked like a shimmering goddess as she danced the part of an apsara, now looked like an ordinary peasant girl — and not even a healthy one at that. More like a shadow puppet than a dancer, she was now.

"Look at you, so thin now," I murmured.

"Look at yourself," she snapped. "Come on, Nakri,

you've got to get up." She took my hands and pulled me upright. A wave of dizziness passed over me, and I put my hand over my eyes. "You'll feel better after some food," Teeda said.

We wouldn't be getting any food for hours, until midday, and that would only be the same bowl of watery rice gruel, thickened with a handful of tapioca flour — no, that wasn't really food.

And before we got even that, we would have to work out in the rice fields — hard work, without rest, under the watchful eyes of the Khmer Rouge cadres — from morning till evening. Still, what else could we do? There was no avoiding it, no escaping it — except through the memory game.

The cadre who supervised us appeared in the doorway now, her black clothes silhouetted against the morning light. In her hoarse, fierce voice, she shouted at us to get up. Early on, she had made it clear to us that we had to obey her every order. "I will watch you," she said, "more closely than a hawk. I have eyes that can look out in every direction, all the time." And so we called her Hawk Eye behind her back.

"Hurry up," Hawk Eye declared now. "You must work

extra hard for the Angkar today. The transplanting must be finished soon."

It was the tail end of the rainy season, and the last of the monsoon wind was blowing softly as we worked, backs bent, transplanting the rice seedlings in paddy fields. Knee-deep in mud, I suddenly stepped on some-thing sharp — a sliver of bamboo, an old fish trap, I couldn't tell what it was. I felt a searing pain up my leg, and collapsed in the middle of the rice fields, scattering a bundle of rice seedlings as I fell. Teeda rushed over to help me, and helped drag me over to the side of the paddy field.

Together we examined the cut on my foot. It was bleeding, and only after she had splashed some muddy water over it, could I see how deep and jagged it was.

Luckily, it was already dusk, and we could make our way back to the shed without drawing too much atten-tion. It hurt to walk on it, especially when bits of gravel and sand worked their way into the cut, but after dinner, Teeda washed it out as best as she could, and tore off a scrap from her scarf to make a bandage for it.

That night, I slept fitfully, tossing and turning, trying

to shake off the pain. When I saw Teeda's tired eyes the next morning, I knew that I must have kept her awake for much of the night.

We went back to work in the fields that day, but by that evening my head was hot, and the foot had swollen quite a bit more. Teeda tried to give me her gruel to eat at dinner, but I couldn't even finish mine.

The next day, I couldn't walk on it at all, and had to hobble along, clinging to Teeda. We were almost the last in line straggling out to the fields, when Teeda paused, and signaled across the fields to somebody.

Another line of workers, all boys, were marching on the other side of the field, and I saw someone detach himself from it, and dart over to us. It was my brother Boran.

"Nakri, what happened?" he asked, falling in step with us.

"She's cut her foot," Teeda said quickly. "It's all swollen, and she's feverish."

"I saw her limping," Boran said. He touched my forehead with his palm, the way my mother used to do when we were sick.

"What do we do?" Teeda asked.

"I know where some wild lemongrass grows. Grandma used to rub it on our cuts, remember? I'll get some."

"And she won't eat," Teeda said, glancing over at me accusingly.

Boran nodded. "I'll try to bring something for her. Tomorrow night, look behind the bamboo clump near your kitchen." And with that he was gone, hurrying to catch up with the other boys in his work camp.

That next evening, Teeda slipped outside to check the bamboo grove. She came back with a tuft of lemongrass, and a package wrapped in banana leaf. Inside was a small fish, roasted on a stick. "Eat," she said, offering it to me.

But my foot was throbbing painfully, and thick pus was starting to ooze out of the wound. I turned my face to the wall, and ignored my sister. She tried to coax me to eat, to massage my back, to unwrap my bandage, but I resisted her attempts to comfort me. "You'll feel better soon," she said. "The harvest will be good, and we'll get more to eat. And maybe we'll get to visit Mother and Yann and Grandma soon, and Pa would be waiting there. Everything will be better," she said. But she did not seem convinced of it herself, and I did not believe her.

I wanted just to be left alone, away from the hurt, the hunger, the constant fear. But my sister would not leave me alone. Instead, she lay down behind me and slipped her arms around my waist, tucking me into the curl of her body, the way my mother used to hold me when I was little. I could feel her breath against the back of my neck, like a light wind.

And then she began to talk, softly against my ear, her words slow and gentle and soothing. And this is the story she told me.

"Once, when I was your age or even younger," she whispered, resting her chin gently on my shoulder so that her mouth was against my ear, "I reached up and touched an apsara."

Touched an apsara? But they were dancers of the heavens, celestial creatures who were not of this world — how could my sister have touched one?

Seeing that she had my attention, Teeda continued. "We were visiting Granny — this was before you were even born — when Ma took me to see Angkor Wat."

Angkor Wat — that ancient temple built of solid stone, almost a thousand years ago. Like every Cambodian, I had of course heard of this sacred site, but I had never been there. Was it so powerfully magical that apsaras still lived there?

"It was nearing sunset, and the shadows were very long," Teeda whispered. "The Angkor Wat Temple was almost deserted, as we walked along the corridors and courtyards."

They were everywhere, Teeda said, and they were beautiful — dancing with their arms raised, fingers bent back to a full arc, and always smiling. "I had started my dance lessons not long before that, and it was as if they were showing me how to dance." Our mother knew the temple well from previous visits, and had led Teeda through the maze of corridors to a special spot, even more sacred than the others. It was where the apsaras first appeared, she said, during the mighty Churning of the Oceans.

And so I heard the age-old story, of the tumultuous struggle between the gods and the demons. At one end, holding the writhing head of a gigantic snake, was a row of demons, their arms straining in unison to pull it. At the other end of the snake, at its tail, was a row of gods, tugging equally hard.

"Like a tug-of-war game," I murmured.

Teeda smiled. "Except that this was in the ocean, and the rope was wound around Mount Mera, which was resting on top of a gigantic turtle." In the pulling of the snake back and forth, the mountain was twirled around and around, churning the waves up into a thick white foam.

As Teeda spoke, I could picture the awesome wildness of it all, the churning waves, the demons grimacing at the gods, the snake writhing between them. "Wasn't it terrifying?" I asked my sister.

Through the thin cloth of her scarf I could feel her fingers digging into my shoulder. For a moment she did not speak. Then she nodded and said, "Yes, it was — but no more than now."

"It's the way the world is now," she said. "Everything churned up, the good and the bad, in a big tug-of-war. But . . ." she relaxed her hold on me, and leaned back to look me in the eyes. "But Nakri, that's where these goddesses first appeared. Out of this terrible struggle they danced their way through the churning waves and flew up to the heavens!"

And they were smiling, my sister said. These apsaras were radiant with grace and joy, and their dancing brought a shining beauty to the storm-darkened world.

"That's what we must be like, little sister," Teeda whispered. "Like the apsara goddesses, we must dance our way up through the storm. Even when — especially when — everything around us is dark, and everybody is fighting each other, we've got to keep our spirit up.

We've got to keep dancing. That's what the apsaras told me, little sister. And that's what I'm telling you now: that if we can only keep the dance alive in our hearts, someday, somehow, we will reach the sunlight and the open sky again."

In the darkness I listened to her voice, and imagined the apsaras joyfully dancing their way out of the churning waves. And I thought of my grandmother weaving at the loom, humming to herself as she sent the shuttle through the taut threads. In her way, she was keeping the dance alive, too. As was my father, when he put his hand on my shoulder, and told me to watch the crescent moon. And my brother and sister now, stubbornly gathering bits of extra food and herbs for me. Each of them was keeping the spirit of hope alive.

Yet it was the apsaras, these radiant goddesses, that most intrigued me. "And . . . and you touched one, an apsara?" I asked Teeda now, my voice hushed in the darkness.

"On the ankle," Teeda said. "So smooth and cool she was, she felt alive even though she was made of stone."

Of course, I thought, the stone goddesses carved on the temple walls. The apsaras, the snake, the gods, and demons were all carved from stone, their vibrant movement caught for one eternal moment on the dark limestone of Angkor Wat.

"If you saw her and touched her, too, this stone goddess," Teeda was saying, "she would tell you the same thing: that you must keep the dance alive, even through the worst storm." My sister looked into my eyes and held my gaze so intently that I could not look away. "Do you hear me, Nakri?" she asked.

I took a deep breath. "I hear you," I said. Then slowly I sat up, and let Teeda feed the morsel of fish to me.

She fed me that, then spooned the rice soup into my mouth as well, as if I were a baby. And she dressed my wound, carefully peeling off the bloodstained bandage where it had stuck onto my skin.

Life was not so horribly bleak after all. I still had my family, and they still cared about me. Even though the Angkar had tried to pull us apart, my sister and I were still bound to each other, with invisible ties stronger than anything the Angkar could snap. And in that I found comfort.

Every day after that, Teeda would check the bamboo grove, and usually there would be a fist-size lump of rice, or a banana, or even some roasted insects, wrapped and tucked away there. How Boran managed to steal the food, and gather the lemongrass, we didn't know. But I admired him for it, even more so now than when he used to come home with medals for running the fastest or jumping the highest in his school.

Each night, Teeda would unbind the bandage and wash out the cut, then gently rub damp lemongrass on it. It stung a little, but seemed to make the swelling go down. I looked forward to the extra tidbits of food from Boran too, and grew a little stronger eating them.

I knew how risky it must be for him to get the food and herbs for me, and after a few days I felt well enough that Teeda thought that I could do without them anymore. She was going to tell our brother, the next time she saw him, not to take that risk anymore.

But the next time we saw him, it was already too late.

That evening, on the way back to our shed, we heard the sound of jeering from the compound between the boys' and girls' work camps. Our group leader pushed us toward the commotion, telling us we should learn a lesson from it. She glared at me, as if the message was directed especially to me.

My heart beating fast, I leaned onto Teeda's arm, and together we hobbled our way over to the crowd that had gathered around a tall stake. Without even seeing him, somehow I knew it would be Boran tied to it.

It was. He was on his knees, both hands bound behind his back and tied to the stake. His head was unbowed, his gaze kept in the distance. Next to me, I heard Teeda stifle a cry. She reached out, as if to run to him, but I grabbed her wrist and held on tight.

"Our food not good enough for you, is it?" a cadre was saying, aiming a kick at Boran's head. "Counterrevolutionary dog! Stealing from the commune's kitchen!" Other cadres came up and joined in the jeering, punching and slapping him. The rest of us stood in silence.

"You'll stay there until you learn to value what the Angkar offers you!" A bowl of watery rice gruel was shoved near him. With a final kick, the cadre turned away, and motioned for us to be dismissed. Boran did not look at him, but kept his head held high.

My throat was so tight I felt as if I was choking. But I did not cry. I stared at the cadre who had kicked my brother, and willed myself to remember the sneer on his face. A wave of hatred, sour and strong, welled up in me.

Even if I had wanted to, I could not have avoided seeing my brother again the next day. We were all forced to walk past him again on our way to the fields.

Still tied to the stake, his head was bent now, so that he seemed to be staring directly into the same bowl of gruel that had been left near him the day before. I wanted to slip out of line and go up to him, hold the bowl to his mouth so he could sip from it, but I didn't dare. Instead, I walked past him, eyes averted, holding tightly onto Teeda because I feared that she might want to do something rash too.

That day spent in the fields was among the longest that I could remember. The sun seemed especially harsh, and I could imagine how its fierce heat beat down on Boran. Why was Boran being punished for something he did for me? Maybe I could offer to take his place at the stake? But suppose that would get us both into more trouble? I did not know what to do, and so I did nothing, and the time dragged by.

When the sun finally set, we were marched back past Boran on our way to our shack. He was looking drawn and weak. Worse, he was straining hard against the ropes, trying to duck his head down low enough to reach the bowl of gruel before him. But he couldn't reach it, and the circle of cadres around him laughed and jeered each time he tried.

I could not stand it anymore.

Breaking free of Teeda, I ran limping up to Boran, and knelt beside him, lifting the bowl of gruel up to his mouth so he could drink from it. Just as he was taking his first sip, a cadre stepped up and kicked the bowl from my hands. Bits of soggy rice splashed onto the dirt.

"You want to be tied up next to him, is that it?" he shouted. "Who are you anyway?"

"His sister," I said.

"There are no sisters under the Angkar!" the cadre exclaimed. "We are all comrades! Do you understand?"

I nodded, not looking at him. Teeda came up and pulled me away, and I did not resist. All that time, Boran kept staring at the bits of spilled rice in the sand. He did not look up at me at all.

They cut him down the next evening, after he had already lost consciousness and they could not torment him anymore. Someone had dragged him into the shade of a tamarind tree, where he was sprawled in a heap, one arm flung over his face. A few flies buzzed around the blood on that wrist, where it had been chafed raw.

Teeda and I hung back from the rest of the workers as they filed past, and when we saw that there were no cadres about, we went over to Boran. The bowl of gruel was still by the stake, dried and emptied. Teeda took the bowl and filled it with well water outside the kitchen, as I sat cradling Boran's head in my lap. Teeda sprinkled some water onto his forehead, which made him stir. We wetted his lips with some water, and held the bowl up to him. In the twilight, I could hear the tree frogs croaking, and the sound of the palm fronds rustling overhead, and it felt almost peaceful, being together with my brother and sister like this.

After a while Boran sighed, and took a sip of water. Then he struggled up, still propped against me, and gulped down the rest of the water in the bowl, in long, deep swallows, barely breathing in between.

Teeda rinsed off the dried blood from his chafed wrists, cleaning them as she had done my cut foot, and I held onto his hand.

"He's going to be all right," Teeda whispered, and I believed her.

Boran did recover, and after several days, was forced to go back to work in the fields. I caught a glimpse of him out there, part of a single file, digging long ditches that cut straight across the paddy fields, without following the natural contours of the landscape, unlike the intricate web of the small old ditches.

For one year we had been living in this village. The

cadres had claimed that we were supposed to be carving a whole new system of irrigation over the countryside, but so far the ditches were dry, and didn't seem to be in use at all. What if these ditches were never really meant to be used at all, but were just made so that young men would become so exhausted from digging them, that they would have no time or energy to rebel against the Angkar?

It was something I had often wondered about, but of course never dared to speak of. Looking at the countless boys, digging and hoeing and hauling baskets of mud from the ditches, I was sure many of them wondered too. Yet none of them challenged the cadres. It was just the Cambodian way, the way we were brought up — to do what we were told, not to question, certainly never to argue, but to swallow our protests and anger and despair, and hope that somehow, someday, things would change, though through no initiative of our own, and we might be freed from this wheel of suffering.

As for Teeda and me, we went back to our routine, waking up at the break of dawn to start work in the fields on an empty stomach, with a break at noon for lunch, which consisted of the usual bowl of rice gruel, and if we were lucky, sometimes a few strips of vegetables stirred into it. Then we would work again, through the long afternoon until past sunset, when we would be marched back to our shed for another bowl of rice soup. There was nothing to break the monotony of it — no singing, no exchange of jokes between the boys and girls, no laughter, no sense of the rhythm of the seasons.

I remember my visits to my grandmother's home, how the villagers effortlessly marked the passing of the seasons with time-worn festivals — the sprinkling of cool water during the dry heat of our New Year celebration, the singing during the transplanting of rice seedlings after the first rains, the offering of new robes to newly ordained monks when the rice was growing, the gay bantering during the harvest times, and the teasing when the rice stalks were being threshed. Times of joy and mourning would be marked too, with music and dancing during wedding feasts, and the solemn chanting of the monks during funerals.

In those days, we had been allowed to feel things, gaiety and sadness both, and we could express those feelings in communal ways. Together, we had been able to mark the passage of time with a kind of rhythmic grace, with song and dance and prayer, so that there was a natural cadence to the way we lived as the moon waxed and waned and the monsoon rains came and went.

There was nothing of the kind now, under this New Society. I was no longer aware of time passing. Instead, it felt as if we were stuck inside some giant machine and forced to repeat the same few actions again and again, with deadening monotony. Twice we were told that it was the anniversary of the glorious liberation of the people of Kampuchea by the Khmer Rouge, and so I knew that three years had passed already since the day we had been forced to leave our lives behind in Phnom Penh and take up this new one. But that bit of knowledge seemed cold and sterile, essentially meaningless.

Perhaps what replaced the natural awareness of time passing was the unnatural fear of being watched, always being watched. There were always Khmer Rouge cadres all around us, patrolling the edges of the fields with a stick in their hands, or sitting in the shade, watch us work. And even when we weren't working, they would silently watch us march, or eat, or bed down to sleep. They even referred to themselves with grim humor as "pineapple eyes," because they had eyes facing every direction, the way the soft yellow flesh of the pineapple was pockmarked in a long, looped spiral with spiky "eyes," so that they could watch us everywhere, all the time.

So we were careful not to do anything that might draw attention to ourselves, or worse, annoy them. Teeda and I tried to work alongside each other, but dared not do it too often because we knew that the cadres didn't like family members to be together.

There was one thing that Teeda did in secret, however, that she knew she would be severely punished for, if she was caught at it. She danced. Not the whole sequence of steps, of course, not even for more than a few minutes or so. But every chance she got, in the twilight when she would be the last one coming in from the fields, or behind the bamboo grove near the river, she would practice. Sometimes I would be with her, and see her furtively adopt the familiar stance of an apsara, heel raised, arms flexed out at right angles, in perfect balance. And always she would bend her fingers as far back as she could, to keep them limber, arching them back toward her elbows in a graceful arc.

At home, she had taken such good care of her hands, soaking them in warm water before flexing her fingers, massaging them with coconut oil, making sure they were smooth and supple. After two years of manual work, though, her hands had thickened with calluses, and her nails were cracked and grimy with dirt. Worse, her fingers had become stiff despite her continual attempts to keep flexing them.

Yet she kept trying. It was her role, she said once. Because she danced the role of the apsara goddess, she had to do whatever she could, no matter how little, to dance her way from the darkness into the light, through the churning waves to the open air.

Even though she kept trying to dance, I could tell it was becoming harder and harder for her to keep supple and limber. Still, she remembered how to perform the dance of the apsaras, and she would practice fragments of it every chance she had.

Her favorite spot to practice was behind the thicket of bamboo, which grew at the edge of the river running between our hut and the fields. There, as she started making the slow, deliberate movements of classical dance, I would watch her, and sometimes try to imitate her.

Always she would encourage me to join her in the dance. Looking back over her shoulder at me, she would say softly, "Come on, Nakri. Just move your arm, like this. And step in my footsteps." Her bare feet would leave imprints in the damp mud, and I would carefully set my own feet inside them. Learning how to angle my toes one way, how to set my heel down in another, I was literally following in her footsteps as we danced.

She would also help me keep my fingers supple, whenever we had a chance. We would take turns binding each other's fingers back with strands of long grass, holding the fingers as far backward toward our arms as possible.

Once, when I flexed the fingers of one hand back with my other, my knuckles cracked so loudly that it startled me. Teeda laughed. "Listen, they're complaining!" she said. "They're saying: You've ignored us too long! We're stiff and hard now."

Then she did the same exercise to flex her fingers, and *crack-crack-crack!* Her knuckles were louder than mine. I giggled.

Teeda grinned. "Silly fingers," she said, pretending to scold them. "How dare you talk to me like that?" She flexed them again, deliberately cracking her knuckles this time. "Be quiet!" she said, frowning at them.

I burst out laughing. It was so good to see Teeda playful again.

"Careful, not so loud," she said, glancing furtively behind her. "Remember Roeun?"

I quieted down at once. Roeun was a graceful young woman who had been Teeda's classmate in the classical dance class, and who had arrived in our cooperative a few weeks after we had. During our orientation meetings, the cadres had asked if anyone had trained as a musician or dancer, because they wanted to start a dance troupe to perform songs praising the Angkar. Roeun had raised her hand shyly, and been told to go to the front of the room, where she was asked a few quick questions. Yes, she had been trained at the Royal University of Fine Arts, she said. Yes, she could dance the classical apsara dance, and could learn to do folk dances. That night, after the meeting, she had been asked to stay behind. We never saw her again. There were rumors that she had been taken out to the forest and clubbed to death, her body tossed into a pit already half filled with rotting corpses.

No, I did not want to be treated like Roeun.

And yet, even knowing this, Teeda refused to give up her dream of dancing as an aspara. She said that sometimes she would just lie awake in the dark, and go through the whole dance in her mind, visualizing each move she would make from beginning to end. The music too she would try and imagine. In her head, she said, it all came together like a beautiful dream.

"Just once," she would say, "I would like to dance it through all the way without interruption, without mistake. Just once — perfectly."

The days passed, each one seemingly endless and indistinguishable from another. Another anniversary of the "Glorious Revolution" was announced, and another cycle of drought before the monsoon rains. Yet what was so glorious about this revolution when we were always hungry and afraid? If anything, the last year had been even more wretched than the one before. Even though we had spent all of our waking hours planting and tending the fields, we never had enough to eat. There was no doubt about it — like everyone else, Teeda and I were thin and getting thinner, weak and getting weaker, and it was becoming ever harder for us to remember back to the happier days of childhood or to look ahead to a brighter future.

We had long since stopped playing the memory game, and in the dull silence of the evenings, I would find myself wondering what had happened to Cambodia. How could a country that before was fertile enough to export rice overseas now have its people in a state of semi-starvation? Was the rice being stored in some vast secret warehouse, to be kept especially for the Khmer Rouge officials? Perhaps it was distributed to parts of Cambodia where hundreds of thousands of people weren't planting rice, but forced to dig ditches, or take up arms against the Vietnam, a country we had been told was now our enemy?

It seemed that there were so many enemies now — apparently not just the U.S. imperialists and the Thai capitalists, but even the Vietnamese Communists were sabotaging "our" revolution. Enemies were everywhere, we were told, and we had to be vigilant, to guard against them over in Vietnam, and closer at hand, among ourselves. Recently even some of the Khmer Rouge cadres themselves had seemed fearful, as if they were being watched over instead of just watching over us. In fact, a few of the more relaxed cadres over in the boys' camp had been replaced by new, harsher ones. And Hawk Eye herself had a hunted look to her sometimes, as if she was afraid of being replaced as well.

If we had thought that our lives had been bleak before, they became even bleaker during this fourth year of the Angkar's rule. The hardest time was always toward the end of the monsoon rains, after the transplanting had been done, but long before the harvest was due. This year it was even worse. Our rice rations had been reduced even more, so that instead of rice porridge we were now getting only rice soup, a thin mixture with a few grains of broken rice at the bottom, and never any extra vegetables at all. And because the paddy fields and streams were drying up, there were no fish or crabs or frogs we could catch to supplement our meals.

Several of the girls who slept in our shed became too weak to work, and they would lie there on their rattan mats, wide eyed and hollow cheeked, in silent suffering. Sometimes they would get taken off to "the hospital," a ward with no doctors, no medicine, and no hope. We all knew, without saying it, that it was only a place to isolate the dying until they died. For a few days after a girl died, or disappeared, there would be an empty spot on the floor where she had slept. But then gradually we would all spread out a little, and the spot would be gone, and there would be no indication that she had ever been there.

With the monsoons over, and the rainwater receding, there were shallow puddles of stagnant water around, where the mosquitoes bred. There were swarms of them, whining around us during twilight and the early evenings. We had no mosquito nets, of course, and although the smoky grass fires we lit every evening helped keep them away, most of us would get bitten during the night, and many would fall sick.

Toward the end of the rainy season, I became feverish, my head burning hot to the touch, while the rest of my body felt horribly cold. I lay there on my mat, my legs drawn up, shivering with cold. No matter how many scarves Teeda managed to borrow and heap on me, I almost convulsed with the cold. Then, as quickly as it began, the chilliness lifted, to be replaced with an all-consuming fiery heat in an erratic pattern typical of malaria.

There was nothing to be done, except to be swept along in the waves of heat and cold, and wait until they subsided and finally ebbed. Teeda sat next to me, but I was barely aware of her.

When I regained enough sense to look for her, I found her curled up next to me, shivering exactly as I had been. She was moaning softly.

So, just as she had wiped me, I dried her damp neck and forehead, then laid a cool wet cloth on her face to bring down her fever. And just as she had saved half of her rice soup for me, I fed her half of mine now, together with her own portion, so that she would have the strength to get better.

But she did not get better. Instead, each bout of fever would build in intensity, lasting longer and following closer to the one before. She became so weak and exhausted that her eyes lost their luster, and she just stared blankly at the ceiling. Eventually, I could tell that she wasn't even fighting the malaria anymore.

Food, I thought. If I got her some good food, some fish or bamboo shoots or white rice, it would give her the strength to keep fighting. I didn't dare ask Boran for help anymore, for fear that he would be punished again. And so I tried to catch some fish on my own. One afternoon, I sharpened a stake and stood knee-deep in the middle of the stream trying to spear a fish. They were much too quick for me, and too small to stab anyway. The next chance I got, I used the safety pin that held my shirt in place. It was one my mother had hastily pinned into a buttonhole for me, when she had noticed that one of my buttons was missing. The other buttons on my shirt had long since come loose and been lost, but that one safety pin was still there, and was a valuable item.

I bent the hook back, threaded an earthworm I had caught onto it, and dangled the hook into the water with a thread ripped loose from my scarf.

It worked! Soon I felt the slightest movement on the hook, and with a sharp tug I yanked the thread up. There was a slippery little fish, no longer than my finger, wriggling on the hook. Quickly, I unhooked it and left it flopping on a pile of weeds. Thank you, Boran, I said silently, for teaching me how to fish during our school holidays.

Twice more, I managed to hook a fish, and probably I should have stopped there. On my fourth try a slightly bigger fish bit into the safety pin and I yanked on it too hard. The thread snapped, and the fish leapt out of the water, then quick as a flash disappeared downstream. My hook was gone.

I sighed. Not for the first time, I found myself wishing that we might have packed some really useful things when we left Phnom Penh. Fishhooks, for instance, nylon string, needles, buttons, plastic bags — it was the simple things that we needed now, not radios and wristwatches.

Still, I had my three little fishes, and these I grilled over some embers that I scraped from the charcoal braziers in the kitchen, and offered them, neatly arranged in a row on a banana leaf, to my sister. I had also plucked a lotus bud that was swaying on its slim stalk anchored in the muddy streambed, and this I offered to Teeda, too, because she used to love practicing with them, holding one aloft as she danced her apsara role.

Looking at the pink blossom in my hand, I thought of the story she had told me, of how apsaras had been created out of the murky water as the gods and demons churned up the ocean. "They're like lotuses, too, these apsaras, keeping alive through the mud and water until they can bloom in the open air." I tucked the thought into the back of my mind, intending to tell it to Teeda when I gave her the lotus.

But she was feverish, and too disoriented to listen. She didn't even seem interested in the grilled fish. "Eat — it will give you strength," I said softly, breaking off a piece of the grilled fish for her. She ate it slowly, chewing it for a long time as if enjoying the taste of it. And I was able to feed her the rest of it, mouthful by mouthful, alternating with spoonfuls of the rice soup. Finally there was only one morsel left. My stomach had been rumbling throughout this, and I wanted that last bit of fish so badly that my mouth was watering.

"Teeda, have you had enough?" I asked her.

She didn't say yes; she didn't say no. Through half-closed eyes she stared at the remaining piece of fish, but made no move to help herself to it.

"Teeda, you've had enough, haven't you? You don't want any more?"

Again she remained silent. Quickly, before she could protest, I popped the morsel into my own mouth and ate. It tasted so good, sweet and flaky the way only fresh fish can taste.

But as soon as I swallowed it, I felt bad that I hadn't given it to her. All those times that she fed me the tidbits of food Boran brought to me, she had never taken a bit of it for herself. Next time, I vowed, I would not touch a bite of it. I would feed it all to her, until she got well.

But the next day, I didn't manage to catch any more fish. Without the safety pin, I didn't have anything to hook them with. I tried making a fish trap, like the ones I had seen my grandfather make once, weaving long reeds loosely together into a kind of funnel which ended in a tightly woven basket. Placed sideways in midstream, it would draw a school of fish into it, the fish swimming along within the reeds into an ever-narrowing band until they were trapped in the basket at the end. As a child, I had been fascinated at how the fish never escaped through the reeds, even though there was space enough for them to swim through easily. Nor did they ever turn around and swim back through the funnel and out again.

"Why not?" I would ask my grandfather, and he would shrug and smile his toothless smile, and say, "They just don't."

"They're so stupid!" I'd say.

And Grandpa would laugh. "No more than people," he said. "People do the same thing too, you know . . . just keep going in one direction, grouped tight together, right into a trap."

I thought back to his words now, and realized what he meant. Hadn't we been like the little minnows, being flushed out of the city, being funneled into an ever-narrower space until here we finally were: trapped?

Teeda, too, was trapped. But unlike the rest of us, she found her own special way of escaping.

It happened early in the morning, when dawn was just a hint of rose in the overcast sky. The glow of the rising sun shone through the open window above her head, glazing the wooden floorboards so that they gleamed like the marble steps going up to the dance pavilion.

Teeda's fever had been raging through the night, and

she had slept only restlessly, tossing her head from side to side on the thin scarf that she used as a pillow. She lifted her head now and looked up at the dawn, and her eyes fell on the stalk of lotus blossom that I had placed near her hand the day before.

"An apsara's wand . . ." she whispered.

I understood. "It's not," I said. "It's just a lotus flower."

But she was past listening to me. With great effort, she reached for the lotus, then stood up. I wanted to pull her back down, but she looked so happy, almost radiant, her face glowing with the morning light.

She knelt, and lifted the lotus blossom over her head, as an offering toward the sky. It was a gesture so natural and yet full of practiced grace that I understood immediately what she was doing. She had slipped into her role as an apsara, a celestial dancer rising from the stormy waves.

Slowly she rose, as smoothly as a strand of willow wafted by a breeze, and started to dance, more beautifully than she had ever danced before. So supple were her arms that it seemed as if she had no joints, no bones even. She held up the lotus to trace graceful arcs in the air. She moved in a fluid circle, pressing each foot soundlessly, heel first, flat onto the ground, ankles crisscrossing to a deliberate rhythm that only she could hear. Was she sidestepping the monsters of the deep, craning her neck gracefully from side to side to watch, wide-eyed, for glimmerings of light in the churning waves? Through it all, she kept her sense of grace and calm, her radiance undimmed by the darkness around her.

I had watched her dance these steps countless times before, and danced them myself next to her, but never had I really understood the spirit of that dance until then. Gaunt and deathly ill she was, my beloved sister, and yet the spirit of the dance still burned in her, giving her an unwavering strength as she moved from the darkness into the dawn light.

Finally, silhouetted sideways against the window, she flexed one knee behind her, tilting the sole of that foot up in the traditional gesture of an apsara flying toward the heaven. She had done it — danced through the dark waters into the light and air!

A deep sigh, like the wind through the rushes, swept through the room. I saw then that the other girls had been watching Teeda dance as well, and had been as enchanted and as deeply moved as I was.

Then another sound, a gasp more than a sigh, made me turn toward the door. Standing there, hands on hips, was Hawk Eye. How long had she been there? How much had she seen?

She strode into the room, and without a word, grabbed Teeda by the arm. "Come with me," she said in a low voice. Docilely, almost in a daze, Teeda started to follow her.

I jumped up. "You can't take her away," I said. "She's sick. Delirious. High fever, see?" Desperately, I took the cadre's hand and placed it on Teeda's forehead. "Please, feel that? See how hot she is?"

The cadre flung my hand off. But I kept on talking, trying to stop her from leading my sister away. "It's because of the fever," I said. "She didn't know what she was doing . . ."

"She knew exactly what she was doing. She was dancing. It's obvious she was trained as a classical dancer!"

"No . . . no, never. She only watched them, once or twice, at festivals. And then . . . then she started imitating them, trying to be like them. That's all . . ."

"Nobody who just watched a few times could dance the way she was doing! She must have been a student in Phnom Penh. What? Tell the truth, or I will beat the both of you."

"No . . . she never set foot in the city. We lived in a village in Siem Reap district all our lives. She's never been to school even. Can't read or write." On and on I jabbered, knowing that the longer I talked, the less likely the cadre was to question Teeda herself. Teeda stood there, dazed, her head cocked to one side as if she was listening not to us but to some distant music.

"She won't try dancing again," I said. "I promise . . . I will watch over her, make sure of it. And nobody . . ." I gestured at the girls in the room, "nobody else will see her dance either. Please, comrade, I promise."

Hawk Eye looked around. Several pairs of bright eyes glowed in the dawn, watching us. I had made my point — there were witnesses here. If Teeda was led away in front of them, they would know it. And it was one of those unspoken facts we all knew, that the Khmer Rouge cadres did not like witnesses. They preferred to take away people in the dead of night, silently, when all others were asleep.

"I will report this to the supervisor," Hawk Eye said. "He will decide the punishment." She let go of Teeda's arm, and turned away. I was able to gently steer my sister back to our corner of the room, where I made her lie down on the mat. For now we were safe, and I felt an immense wave of relief.

All the energy had drained out of Teeda after the dance. There was a slight sheen on her face, from the dawn's sunlight glistening on her sweat. Carefully I wiped it dry, dabbing at her smooth skin with the home-spun scarf that Grandma had given her. Weakly, Teeda's fingers fluttered for it, trying to grasp the end of the scarf. I draped the soft material across her chest and wound it loosely over her hands, so that she would have something to hold. That seemed to calm her, and she closed her eyes and drifted into a deep sleep, with her breathing slow and rhythmic.

Through the lingering dawn, I watched over her. Aside from her breathing, and the slow rise of the sun across the cloudy sky, the world seemed to stand still. I felt a strange, calm joy, in just being there, with my sister and the moon. It was as if nothing else mattered, or even existed, outside of us.

Sometime toward morning I must have fallen asleep, slumped against the wall. When I woke up, strong sunlight was streaming through the window, and the rest of the girls in the room were already bustling about, preparing for the day's work in the fields. I could hear Hawk Eye's shrill voice ordering us to hurry up.

She was standing directly over me, with her face in shadow. "Shut that window," she said.

Groggily, I got up and started to pull the shutters closed. Then I stopped. "My sister . . . can't we leave it open? She likes the fresh air."

Hawk Eye grunted. "Shut the window," she repeated. "And keep it shut." Something about the tone of her voice, the flat cruelty of it, sent a chill through me. I looked down at Teeda, and understood.

She had gone — nothing remained but the shell of what she was. Like the hollow cocoon that silkworms chew a hole through and emerge from, her thin body lay outstretched on the mat, empty. I touched her hand — it was cool. Gently I pried her fingers off the black scarf and pulled it free. They would take her away soon enough, I knew, and I would never be able to touch her again. But her soft, old scarf, I thought — at least that I could keep. I wound it once, twice around my neck, feeling almost as if Teeda was giving me a hug as I did so.

And then I closed the window, shutting out the fresh air and the sunshine.

From then on, I shut myself off too. I forced myself not to look anywhere but directly in front of me. I forced my mind not to think of anything but what directly affected me. When the other girls marched off to work in the fields, I walked along after them, training my eyes on the feet of the girl directly in front of me. When they ate, I ate. When they lay down, I lay down. Step by step, stroke for stroke, breath by breath, I lived alongside the others, and did not look up, and did not think of anything beyond the next moment, and did not feel anything but hunger and fatigue.

And each night, I would lay my head down on the scarf that Teeda had used for a pillow, and fall into a heavy, dreamless sleep.

Part Three

*O*ne morning, Boran came into the girls' shed and shook me awake.

Looking at him sleepily, I pushed him away. "You . . . you're not allowed in here!" I mumbled. If he left quickly, maybe Hawk Eye wouldn't see him.

But Boran did not leave. "It's all right," he said. "They're gone. All of them . . . even Hawk Eye," he added.

Some of the other girls in the shed were awake now, and sitting up to listen too. Through the open doorway, the half light of dawn filtered in. "What happened?" one of them asked.

"The rumors were true," Boran answered. "The Vietnamese army really did invade Cambodia. They've taken over Phnom Penh and are fanning out all over the countryside now. The Khmer Rouge were no match for them — they're not even putting up a fight anymore. I saw the top cadres all climbing onto a truck that came for them just now. And the lower-ranking ones are just running away!"

"Boran, are you sure?" I asked. My voice shook.

"Would I be here if I wasn't?" he retorted. "Now come ON!"

So I got up and followed him, flinging Teeda's old scarf across my shoulder as I went. Without a backward glance, I walked through that open doorway of the shed, and out into the early morning.

The air was fresh and cool. In the sky was the faintest tinge of dawn, and the tips of the palm fronds were already brushed with gold. There was no one in sight — no cadre, that is. A few children were wandering around, scavenging for food in the kitchen. There was no one to stop them, no one to order them off to the fields. It was so quiet — a good kind of quiet, one that didn't feel as if it would be broken abruptly.

It had taken almost four years, but finally someone had punched a hole in the fish trap. It was January 1979, and the Vietnamese army had crossed the border into our country, and sent the Khmer Rouge running. Overnight, the almighty Angkar had dissolved, its network of cadres ripped apart like so many spiderwebs. And there was nothing and nobody to hold us back anymore — just a gaping hole we could all slip through, back out into the open again.

In the distance, the muted explosions of artillery and gunfire that we had been hearing the last few nights had stopped. A flock of white egrets winged across the fields, and disappeared into the horizon.

"This way! Come on!" Boran said, tugging at me impatiently.

Behind the kitchen, in the same clump of tall bamboo where he used to hide the tidbits of food for me when I was sick, Boran now dragged out a bicycle. I gasped. He must have stolen it from one of the cadres.

"There's more!" he said, pointing to a bag of rice, a machete, and finally, a hard brown lump of something.

"What's that?" I asked, as he handed it to me.

He grinned. That flash of mischief I had known so well was back. "Try it," he said.

Cautiously I licked the brown rock in my hand. It was sweet.

Sugar! It was a lump of brown sugar from sugar palm

trees. I licked it again and again — it was so wonderful to taste sweetness again.

That whole morning tasted sweet.

Boran got on the bicycle and I climbed onto the seat behind him, holding onto his waist with one arm and the bag of rice with the other. I was surprised at how close to the ground my legs dangled. I thought of that last time I rode behind my father on his motorcycle, and how I had to be lifted onto the seat. In the four years since, I must have grown quite a bit taller.

In less time than it takes to tell it, we had bicycled out of the area that we had been confined to for so long. We left behind sheds, the fields, the ditches, the surrounding forest, keeping to a bike path outside the forest, because Boran didn't want to run into any of the Khmer Rouge soldiers that he thought might well be hiding there. "But what if we are caught by the Vietnamese soldiers?" I asked. They had guns; they rode around on big military trucks — they were now clearly in control. But although they didn't speak our language, they smiled and seemed approachable, even friendly. Already we had seen them slow down their trucks, and offer to give rides to the sick or elderly who were walking along the road.

"The Viets? What about them?" Boran grunted. "Nothing could be worse than the Angkar." And with that I had to agree.

Later that morning, we saw more of these Vietnamese soldiers in their green uniforms, and they didn't seem to be a threat at all. In fact, they were helping some villagers put out a fire that was burning down a rice storage barn, organizing a bucket brigade to splash water from a nearby well onto the flames. We stopped and asked an old woman about it, and she said that the Khmer Rouge had set the storage barn on fire before they ran off, so that no one else would get at the rice. Boran nodded grimly. It sounded like something they would do.

Yet it hardly mattered what they did anymore. We were going home. That was the last set of orders from Angkar, Boran told me. A few of the cadres had rushed through his shed that morning, waving their weapons, and said, "Go home! All of you, go home!"

As we biked along, we saw dozens, then hundreds of other people on the move, some on bicycles like us, but most on foot. In small groups, or singly, empty-handed or with scraps of their belongings bundled in cloth sacks, in silence or talking together.

If someone had punched a hole in a fish trap, I thought, the minnows crowded inside would probably swim out the hole in dribs and drabs like we were doing, darting every which way, just getting used to the wide world outside the trap. That's how we all were, really, like minnows darting out of a torn trap.

Everyone was on the move, making their way back to where they thought "home" was, or hoped it might still be.

How strange, I thought, that the Angkar's last order would be the only one we would follow willingly. Go home? Oh, we certainly will, Hawk Eye. Just watch us! I laughed out loud, and took another lick at the lump of palm sugar.

By nightfall, we had reached the outskirts of Phnom Penh. The city lay between the cooperative where we had been, and our grandparents' village where we hoped to find our parents, little Yann, and our grandparents. Boran suggested we make a detour into Phnom Penh, just to see what was there. I understood — he didn't want to sound too hopeful, but if we found our old home there, intact and still livable, wouldn't it make sense for us all to move right in again, and take up where we left off? Four years instead of three days later, but still we might have our old lives back. I wished with all my heart that we could do that, and I knew Boran did too, but neither of us dared talk about it. It was too fragile a dream.

The curving sweep of the Wat Phnom temple roof was the first thing I recognized — set high on the hill above the city. In the twilight it gleamed a dull gold, like the wing tips of the egrets I had seen that morning.

We were on asphalt now, one of the main roads leading into Phnom Penh. Twice, convoys of military trucks had rumbled past us, going in the opposite direction, but they had not bothered us. Still, Boran thought we should wait until dark before we went farther into the city.

It was pitch black when we entered the city. There had been Vietnamese soldiers guarding the roads, but in the dark we slipped past them easily, by going off into the fields, and then onto small back roads.

It did not look or feel like Phnom Penh at all. There were no lights, no noise, no people. The asphalt was under our feet, and slabs of concrete in the buildings loomed up, but otherwise we might as well have been back in the countryside, so silent and still was it. At first

I thought it had been recently deserted — that the Khmer Rouge must have abandoned it when the Vietnamese came in — but then we saw that the entire city had been unlived in, for years and years. Tall weeds grew everywhere, in gardens and courtyards, from cracks on the balconies of houses and potholes on the road. Shells of burned-out cars and buses littered the streets, and weeds grew from between their wheels and from the upholstery.

Walking side by side, wheeling the bicycle, we made our way deeper into the city, heading to where our house was. We passed rows of shop houses, which in the old days used to sell groceries or books, clothes or jewelry, their shop fronts usually barred at night by sliding metal gates. Those had been pried open, and left gaping. We peered inside one of them. It was filled with shoes, sandals, boots, sneakers, even stiletto heels, heaped haphazardly up to the ceiling, huge moldy mounds of them.

In another house were piles of television sets, some of the screens cracked, the floor littered with broken glass, black wires snaking out from them. Elsewhere there was a building full of refrigerators, another jammed with suitcases, another full of clocks.

Was this the Angkar's way of trying to make sense of

a lifestyle that it could not understand and had no use for? They had descended into our city, emptied it of its people, sorted through the artifacts left behind, then lost interest and gone away.

And then we were home — or at least, in the house that used to be home. The gate was hanging at an odd angle, as if it had been ripped loose. Weeds as tall as my shoulder covered the garden. Boran walked through it, to the front door, but I stayed outside. It wasn't my home anymore. I felt like I would be trespassing. I watched Boran disappear into the front room, imagined him walking up the stairs, down the hallway to my old bedroom.

My bedroom — the last time I had been in there, morning sunlight had filtered in from the mango tree outside and cast dappled shadows on my mosquito net. The image was as sharp and clear in my mind as a photograph. And I remembered the photo album that I had hidden in the bureau there — hadn't I vowed to come back and retrieve it? Could it still be there?

On an impulse, I ran into the house and groped my way up the stairs, feeling my way down the corridor and into my room. Incredibly enough, things seemed pretty intact. My bed was still there, next to Teeda's, although the mosquito nets over them were torn and grimy, hanging down in shreds like huge cobwebs. I made my way over to the bureau, and pulled open the top dresser. It seemed smaller, now that I didn't have to reach up for it on tiptoe anymore. Inside, gleaming in the dust, was the crystal globe that Teeda had treasured. I started to scoop it up, and stopped. Cool and smooth to the touch, it felt almost like I was about to hold my sister's hand. That would have been more than I could bear. Quickly I pushed it aside, and reached for the photo album next to it.

The cover of the album was moldy, but the photos were still pasted onto its pages. I picked it up, and something fell out. It was the letter that a foreign friend of Father's had sent him, with a photo that he had taken of our family enclosed inside. The foreign stamps on the envelope looked as colorful as ever, and the handwriting on it was still legible. I could see my father's name, "Mr. Hoon Sokha," followed by our street address. I took out the photograph from the envelope, and in the fading light I could see our family as it once was, with Ma and Pa in the middle, surrounded by us children, gathered in front of our hibiscus hedge. Just a stone's throw away from where I was standing now, I thought — yet how very far away it all seemed!

Carefully I slipped the photograph back into its envelope, and tucked it inside my shirt. Then I went back downstairs.

Boran was already at the bicycle, waiting for me.

"Did you find anything?" he asked.

I hesitated. Somehow, I wanted to keep the photograph all to myself for now. Time enough to share it later, after I had pored over it alone. "Not much," I said.

"I didn't either," he said.

"What do we do now?" Our voices sounded hollow, like ghosts mumbling in the darkness.

"We leave," Boran said, and turned to walk away.

I stood there a moment longer, looking at the silhouette of the house. Then gently, I pulled the gate shut, and followed my brother down the deserted street.

Wheels, I thought, were truly amazing things. Sitting comfortably on top of them, we were able to cover more ground in one day than we could have walked in four or five. Because I was gliding along head and shoulders above the people on foot, the two-hundred-mile trip northwest from Phnom Penh to where my grandparents' village of Phum Spean Tnaot was in Siem Reap province felt easier than we had expected.

It was still a time of mass confusion, and the roads were teeming with people who didn't seem to know what would happen next. But at least there were no Angkar to tell us what to do now. Most of the people were, like Boran and me, headed back to some home where they hoped to meet up with family members. Others were tagging along after the Vietnamese army, hoping for handouts and protection in case the Khmer Rouge returned. Everything was in a state of flux — in fact, there was a feeling of lightheartedness in not knowing what might happen next. Each of us could mull about what we might want to do now, rather than have to follow orders for every small step. There was no violence, nobody bullying anyone else.

By late afternoon of the sixth day, we had arrived at Phum Spean Tnaot, my grandparents' village. Nothing seemed to have changed, except that my favorite mango tree seemed shorter, its branches more spindly and closer to the ground. We rode past the temple, and I slowed down, remembering how the cadres had smashed the Buddha statue under the temple eaves. The statue was still there, but had been toppled onto its side, broken into several pieces. In the twilight, the door to the main temple was ajar, hanging lopsided inside from one hinge. A few stray chickens hopped over the doorjamb and a buffalo was inside the temple, flicking its muddy tail onto the murals painted inside. The Khmer Rouge had turned our shrine into a barn.

Ahead of me, Boran was ringing his bicycle bell as he approached Grandma's house. I held my breath as we rode the final stretch down the winding dirt path. What if it was like our house in the city? What if Grandma's house turned out to be just as empty and abandoned? What if nobody was there anymore?

And then I heard it, the sweet rhythm of my grand-mother's shuttle, *click-clack, click-clack,* as it threaded back and forth through her loom. Boran jumped off his bike, and rushed over to her, calling out to her.

She looked up at him, her eyes vague with age, as he knelt down at her feet, so that his head was lower than hers. She reached out and touched his cheek.

"Grandma, it's me," he said. "I'm back!" She stroked his hair, felt the contours of his cheeks, his chin, his neck, and her face lit up with a wide smile.

"Boran, child — I can't believe this . . . ," she crooned.

And then I was kneeling beside her too. Eagerly she touched me, her fingers smoothing out the wrinkles from the scarf around my hair. She lifted the cloth and examined it, recognizing it as the cloth she had woven for my sister. In a voice tremulous with hope, she bent over me and whispered, "Teeda, my little beauty. Teeda, is it really you?"

I felt my throat constrict. "No, Grandma," I said. "I'm sorry — it's just me, Nakri."

And so our reunion was like countless others: the tears of joy were mixed with tears of sorrow, the laughing merging with the weeping. For every one of us who rejoiced at finding a loved one alive, there was someone else who mourned the dead. And those who had survived often felt as if we didn't deserve to, that we had taken the place of someone more worthy who had died. I saw how my grandmother had tried to hide her disappointment that I was not Teeda — her graceful, gentle, good-natured Teeda — and I couldn't blame her. Why should I have returned, when Teeda did not?

My grandmother wiped the tears from her cheeks with her gnarled fingers, and she was smiling now. "Boran and Nakri, at long last! Your mother never gave up hope that you'd come back. And here you are, bigger and taller even. I must call her . . . let everyone know you're back."

She got up from the loom, and hobbled to the steps leading upstairs.

One by one, she called them by name: my mother, Bouth, my uncle Kem, my aunt Pen, my cousins Pum and Soth, my little brother, Yann.

But not my grandfather.

And not my father.

My father had never returned, Ma told us later that night, as we sat huddled around a kerosene lamp on the veranda upstairs. There was a plate of little coconut cakes, made from grated coconut, sticky rice, and flakes of palm sugar from the lump I brought back with me. It was such a special treat that no one ate them. It seemed enough for now just to have them there, in the center of the circle of family. I sat tucked between Ma and Grandma, leaning sometimes against one shoulder, then against the other, feeling so safe.

"There were rumors at first," Ma said, "that your father had been sent far up north, to the jungles near the Laotian border, to some 're-education camp,'" but the months passed, and there had been no sign of him. "I didn't dare ask too often," Ma continued. "We weren't supposed to think about our family, you know. Just the Angkar."

"We know," Boran said.

Then different rumors began to filter down. That the men who had been led away weren't coming back. That they had been taken out to the forest, where they were told to dig a large hole. That they were shot, or clubbed, or axed, to death, falling into the mass grave that they had dug for themselves.

Rumors like that we had heard too. But I had never been able to bring myself to think of my father's life ending like that, much less talk about it. Now we were talking about it, and it felt as if with each word, we were throwing more lumps of clay to bury him.

Ma said that one day, she saw a cadre wearing my father's sandals. They were distinctive ones, leather straps with square metallic buckles. "I confronted him about it. Asked him where he had gotten his sandals," Ma said. The cadre had tried to brush her aside, then gotten angry when she insisted on knowing. "I would have kept after him. I was so upset, seeing Hoon's sandals on his feet, but your little brother dragged me off."

She paused and held Yann closer to her. He had

grown taller, but it seemed that the childish fat he used to have had gone into stretching him out, with nothing left to spare, so that he was all skin and bones.

Yet compared with us, their lives had been relatively easy. Most of the village farmers, like my uncle Kem, had been left to plant their rice crop as they had all along, except that the harvests had to be handed over to the Angkar, who then doled a part of it back to them. Still, there had been no massive work projects, and some of the families had remained intact, with the younger children allowed to stay on with their parents.

Food had gotten very scarce during the past year, and many of the villagers — especially the old and the young — had starved to death. Grandpa had weakened before the last harvest and died a few months later.

So here we were, the ones who were left. I looked around the tight family circle. There were eleven of us. I counted the little coconut cakes on the plate — there were fourteen.

"Eat," Grandma said now, handing the plate around. We each helped ourselves to a piece, and when the plate was put back in the center of the circle, there were still three little cakes left on it — the ones meant for my father, my grandfather, and my sister Teeda. In the flickering light of the kerosene lamp, we stared at the three cakes and ate in silence.

For the next few weeks, there was no talk of any long-term plans. What to do, where to go, how to live — all the big questions were set aside as we talked about small things, things that were not beyond our control.

"Shall we have fish curry or lemongrass soup for dinner?" Ma would ask.

"Both!" Aunty Pen would reply, and they would both laugh in delight.

It had been so long since I had anything but rice soup for dinner that anything else was a treat. But what was even better was eating together, as a family, helping each other to morsels of food, asking and replying to each other's questions — sharing because we wanted to, not because we were told to.

In fact, the best part of being part of a family again was the sharing. And the sense of safety, of feeling that I could let down my guard and relax, because there would be others nearby who would take care of me.

And I could take care of others too, without worrying that some Hawk Eye would interfere. My little brother,

Yann, was very weak when I first came back, his hair brown and dry, falling out in tufts. His arms and legs were stick-thin, and his belly had bloated up so much his belly button bulged out. He was hardly able to walk. Such a difference from the lively little boy I remembered, that I could barely recognize him.

Yet my grandmother insisted he was not sick. "There's nothing wrong with him that some good food won't fix," she said.

And so I took care of him. It was a joy to feed him, to spoon thin rice gruel into his mouth, and watch him get stronger with every spoonful. Mother chopped up bits of fish and eggs, and sometimes even pork and green vegetables, to mix with his gruel; we called it his medicine, and it seemed to work.

I could tell he was getting better. His stomach became less bloated, and he could walk a few wobbly steps on his own. Every night I would sleep next to him, hearing his breathing near me, and feeling the warmth of his small, smooth back tucked against me. Sometimes, as I was drifting off to sleep, I would catch a glimpse of our mother nearby, just standing there, watching over us, and I would feel so safe.

*   *   *

With each passing day, we would see more and more people on the move. Whole families in oxcarts, single men on foot, clusters of ragged children — there was a constant stream of people coming and going. At first, Boran and I would stand by the roadside, and watch them pass. Some of them would pause under the big tamarind tree to drink from the clay urn we kept filled with fresh water. Whenever he could, Boran would draw the people into conversation, and glean bits of information from them, rather like the children gleaning rice from the harvested fields alongside the road, sifting through the threshed stalks for stray grains.

There was a lot of talk about the Thai border. Apparently an active trade had sprung up, with Cambodian smugglers trading bits of jewelry for things like batteries, cooking oil, and cloth from Thai merchants on the border. These items would then be brought back into Cambodia, to be sold at stalls that were sprouting up everywhere, especially in towns close to the border like Sisophon.

Soon individual peddlers roamed the countryside, their baskets brimming with soap and incense and calendars — things that had seemed so ordinary before but that were now priceless treasures. One man even sold spools of thread of cotton, polyester, and silk, all in a range of rainbow colors. Grandma's eyes glowed when she saw them. She had been weaving with nothing but black thread these last four years.

Since the Khmer Rouge had destroyed all money, we traded two chickens and five ripe papayas for ten spools of bright red, orange, and yellow thread. Grandma fingered the thread as if it were pure gold.

It was wonderful the way bright colors were appearing again. I saw a girl wearing a blouse of bright pink, and a blue sarong with a zigzag of green and yellow on the border. Like an orchid in full bloom, she was, in the middle of a parched landscape.

Not only color, but music too, came back into our lives. Most of the musicians had died or been killed under the Khmer Rouge, but somewhere in the village, the son of an old musician had dug up the bamboo slats of a xylophone that his father had made, and strung them together, and was tapping melodies out on it again. Another man made a long drum out of buffalo hide and a hollow tree trunk, and someone else had a reed pipe. Around campfires at night, and under shade trees by day, you could hear people singing old folk songs, and clapping along with the music.

*　　*　　*

Refreshing as these changes were, we still realized how insecure our lives were. The skirmishes between the Khmer Rouge and the Vietnamese soldiers could flare up again. And we had no way of supporting ourselves. Once we had consumed our meager supply of rice, and eaten up the few scrawny chickens around, what would we live on?

Talk of crossing to Thailand, over the border, became widespread. There were rumors that foreigners had set up huge distribution points on the Thai-Cambodian border, where sacks of rice and tools and medicine were being given away for free.

Boran kept gathering information. He learned that young men like himself had been slipping back and forth across the border, not just smuggling luxury goods back from the Thai side, but guiding Cambodians over to Thailand as well, for a fee.

It would be a dangerous trip, he told us, traveling over terrain that had been heavily land-mined by the Khmer Rouge, and patrolled both by Vietnamese troops on our side, and Thai soldiers on the other. And it would be expensive too, as the smugglers charged about one gram of gold per person to guide them across.

But once across the border, Boran had heard, there would be sacks of rice — white, milled rice! — handed out free, and medicine, and maybe even tools, like hoe heads and fishnets and rope. Why not try to cross into Thailand, and stock up on food and tools? Boran suggested to us.

Uncle Kem agreed. There was nothing to be gained by all of us staying, he said. The rice that had been just harvested was almost all gone, either destroyed by the retreating Khmer Rouge soldiers, or consumed by the people. Nor was there enough rice seed for the next planting, or enough buffaloes and ploughs to work with, Ma added. The long years of civil war and then after that the devastation under Pol Pot had depleted all our resources. What would we live on if we stayed?

What if the Khmer Rouge soldiers came back? What if the Vietnamese became more strict and prevented us from leaving? Wasn't it better to leave now, when we still had a chance to?

The discussion lasted late into the night. I was getting sleepy, but was determined to listen because all this concerned me as well. Besides, I liked being allowed to stay up with the grown-ups instead of being ordered off to bed. And so I sat quietly in the corner, and listened.

Like the pattern of stripes and zigzags that emerged on the bright sarong that Grandma was weaving on her loom, a hopeful plan gradually took shape within our family. We would go to the border, and see for ourselves what was there. We hoped we would be able to stockpile enough supplies to come back here in time to plant a new crop of rice. After that, who could tell? If the rains were good and the countryside remained peaceful, perhaps we could stay on here for a while, maybe even return to our house in Phnom Penh and resume life there. One thread at a time, Grandma said, one day at a time. As for herself, she declared that she was too old to make such a trip. She would remain at her loom, weaving her sarong, and wait for us to return. My cousin Rea, who was six months pregnant with her first baby, would stay behind with her.

The rest of us, Uncle Kem and his wife and three children, his son-in-law, and Boran, Yann, Ma, and myself, would join a group of four other families from the village who would also be going. It was safer, we had been told, to travel in a large caravan than in small numbers.

Once the decision had been made, we started preparations for the trip. I helped my cousins husk a sack of rice that we would take along for the trip, stepping on a large wooden log that pounded at the rice grains in a hollowed-out tree trunk, like a giant mortar and pestle. Then we winnowed the light husks away, and carefully packed the husked rice into a coarse sack. Meanwhile, my mother and aunt cooked beans, salted some duck eggs in brine, and ground cornmeal. Uncle Kem dragged out his old oxcart, and he and Boran replaced the axle and repaired a broken wheel. As for our belongings, we had so little left that it took no time at all to pack them into cloth bundles, which we stowed with some pots on the oxcart.

And then we were ready to go.

Grandma, of course, did not say good-bye. Instead, she was at her loom, her head bent over the shuttle, her bare feet working the pedals. I stood before her, wanting to say good-bye but not knowing how. Sensing my awkwardness, she stopped her rhythmic working of the loom, and looked up at me.

"This scarf, it's for you," she said. "Can you wait until I finish it?"

Such lovely squares of overlapping gold and red — it was like the sunset seen through a prison. I fingered the plain black-and-white checkered one that had once belonged to Teeda, and I knew that I would never replace that one with anything new. Besides, the others were impatient to be off. So I shook my head and said, "Thank you, Grandma," I said. "But I'd better come back for it."

If she did not believe me, she did not say so. Silently, she lowered her head, and sent the shuttle shooting across the loom again.

For a moment I stood there and took a long look at everything. A patch of sunlight splashed onto the loom, making the fiery colors of the cloth glow. I had swept the dirt floor just that morning, and could still see the faint marks of the broom in the dust. I thought of my father's pair of glasses, hidden in the dirt under the far corner of the loom. Would they still be there? Should I take them with me?

I walked over to the spot, and pried loose the dirt with a stick. Yes, there it was, that small tube of bamboo. I pulled it up, and carefully took out Pa's glasses from it. Perfectly intact, the lenses still clear and clean. It was almost like touching my father again. For a moment I wanted so much to keep them, and take them along with me. Then I realized that the sound of the shuttle had stopped, and that my grandmother was watching me.

Without a word I placed the pair of glasses on the

wooden bench next to her. In case he comes back, I prayed. They don't have to be hidden anymore, these glasses — they can be right here in the open, waiting for him, in case he comes back.

Behind me I could hear the slow grinding of the cart wheels as they started to roll. I ran toward the cart, and behind me I could hear the shuttle of the loom starting up again, patiently clicking away.

The journey to the border area was easy, even relaxed. We joined a stream of other villagers on the wide, paved highway, some in oxcarts like ourselves, others pushing wheelbarrows of belongings, still others with only bundles tied onto sticks. But we were all moving of our own free will, not forced along at gunpoint as when we'd been evacuated by the Khmer Rouge. There was an almost festive atmosphere, as children ran between groups and we chatted and exchanged news and gossip with other families along the way.

Toward the end of the second day, as our caravan approached the temple of Angkor Wat, my uncle suggested that we stop and spend the night there, taking shelter amidst the ancient ruins.

Mother beamed. "That's fine," she said, and squeezed my hand. I could feel her suppressed excitement. Neither my mother nor I had ever seen this temple, famous throughout Cambodia and even the world!

Before long we could see the enormous spires of the ancient temple of Angkor Wat rising like sharp peaks out of a vast plain, encircled by a set of walls, which was in turn ringed by a moat. My mother gasped.

"Built hundreds and hundreds of years ago," Uncle Kem announced.

Ma nodded. "About eight hundred," she said. "Under the reign of King Suryavarman II."

My uncle looked at Mother sharply. He could never quite get used to how educated his younger sister had become.

"The spires are supposed to symbolize the peaks around Mount Meru, home of the gods," my mother continued calmly, "at the center of the world, and the courtyard walls are the surrounding mountains, while the moat represents the ocean at the edge of the world."

As we approached the enormous structure, my mother would point out the ceremonial gateways with their balustrades, and the buildings alongside, which were supposed to have housed the court library and the carvings on the walls.

Uncle Kem pulled his oxen to a stop at the moat, and got off. "Might as well stop here for the night," he said.

My mother and I climbed off the cart and wandered around. It was cool and quiet, and, in the lengthening shadows, the only movement was the shimmer of the Angkor Wat towers reflected in the moat. As we walked through an open gateway toward the inner walls, I thought I saw other people moving in the shadows. I walked closer, and saw that they were figures carved out of stone, as if emerging from the wall.

There were farmers planting rice, fishermen in their boats casting nets, women selling baskets of fruit in market stalls, even a scene where men gathered around a cockfight. So Cambodians like ourselves had lived ordinary lives much like ours, even a thousand years ago? Where were they now? Had their energy gone into building this massive structure? And was this what the peak of our long civilization had come to — this empty shell?

We walked on, away from the setting sun, so that its long rays slanted ahead of us as we threaded our way further in, to an inner courtyard. The shadows were getting longer, and just when I thought that we might be lost, Ma stopped and took a deep breath.

"There it is," she said.

There in front of us now was the scene depicting the Churning of the Ocean, just as Teeda had described it to me that night at the work camp when I was sick. A huge panel of stone carvings stretched more than one hundred feet long. It showed a row of demons gripping the head of a gigantic snake; gods pulled from the other end, caught in a perpetual struggle thousands of years old, their stone faces still grim, their stone bodies still straining. It was even more awesome that Teeda had described. Trapped under the feet of the massive gods and demons were creatures of the deep — fishes and crocodiles and lionlike Singhas — mired in the mud.

Yet, rising above this fearful turmoil, was a line, a lovely wave, of graceful apsaras, the goddesses of stone, and sure enough, they were dancing their way up to the sky. Fingers arched, feet flexed, arms gracefully lifted, they looked so full of joy.

What had Teeda said? That the turmoil in this Churning of the Ocean was exactly what Cambodia was going through today, with two sides locked in such an awful battle that huge waves of violence swept up to engulf the world. And yet she had, like these apsaras, managed to rise above it all, and danced till the very end.

Like she had done, I stretched up my hand and touched one of these apsaras on the ankle. As I felt the cold, hard stone under my fingers, I missed my sister so terribly that it felt as if my heart was being ripped out from inside me.

Abruptly I turned and walked away, blinded by tears. Then, rounding a doorway, I stopped short. I had caught a glimpse of something that was at once incredibly strange and yet very familiar.

There, shimmering in the doorway, was my sister, Teeda, resplendent in a white apsara gown, silver bracelets on her slender wrists, and a heavy necklace under her delicate collarbones. Crowned by an ornate headdress, her face was smooth and innocent of suffering, just as it had been before the harsh years in our work camp. She looked poised to dance.

Teeda, I called to her silently. But she did not move.

Desperately I stepped toward her and reached out — but she was gone. I blinked, and Teeda had melted into the stone. In her place was a carving of a stone apsara, which looked so much like her that it seemed as if she had stepped out of it for a magical moment before being absorbed back into the stone again.

Tentatively I went and touched this stone goddess,

running my hands along the apsara's arm, and it felt like my sister's arm, smooth and round and firm. Stone or spirit, goddess or sister, I didn't care. It felt as if Teeda were still with me.

Mother walked up to the stone figure I was staring at. For a long moment Ma said nothing. Then she reached out and cupped the dancer's round shoulder, and she whispered, "Tell me now, child, did Teeda die in pain?"

I stared at the stone dancer, and took a deep breath. I did not want to talk about it, could not. Yet my mother was waiting for an answer. Hesitantly, I touched the stone cheek, and traced the smooth curve of her chin down to her neck. "She was dancing," I said. "At the end, she danced the apsara role. All of it. Perfectly." The stone was cold and hard under my fingertips, and I let my hand drop back down to my side. I did not want to touch her anymore, this forever-young stone dancer. Unlike my sister Teeda, she was not warm and soft.

That night, we set up camp in the fields near the temple ruins. Some of us slept under the cart, others on the bare boards on top of it. It was just toward the end of the rainy season, but the sky remained clear during those nights, and I slept under the stars.

*　　*　　*

The next morning, we approached the market town of Sisophon, where the roads from two other areas of Cambodia converged. Beyond that, the highway crossing over to Thailand would be heavily guarded, we were told, with so many checkpoints on it that it would be impossible to cross over that way.

Instead, we would have to abandon our oxcart and make our way on foot, first through the stubbled rice fields, then through bamboo thickets into a strip of overgrown jungle that had been heavily mined by the Khmer Rouge years ago, and was heavily patrolled now, by the Vietnamese troops on one side and Thai soldiers on the other. Nobody, it seemed, wanted to let Cambodians out of Cambodia.

It was through this strip of jungle that we would need a guide. As prearranged, a lanky young man was waiting for us on the night of the new moon, at a clearing where other families had collected as well. Mother handed my silver link belt over to him, and he weighed it casually in his hand before pocketing it.

Single file, he told us quietly, each one in the footsteps of the one before him. To step off the trail might mean immediate death, if we stepped on a land mine. No talking, no rest stops, no lights. Babies had to have their mouths stuffed with cloth, so they couldn't cry out. Yann slipped his little hand into mine. I was glad he wasn't a baby anymore.

A light drizzle began as we made our way up a hillside overgrown with bushes and vines. It was hard not to stumble over the tree roots and vines made slick with mud and rain. Once, I fell down, and landed clumsily off the trail, one arm stretched out to break my fall. But nothing happened — no mine, no explosion. The guide did not slow down.

Once, I heard Boran's sharp intake of breath. He was immediately in front of me, and I almost bumped into him, he stopped so abruptly. Then he started walking again, and I saw what had stopped him. Part of a corpse — almost a skeleton, actually — was splayed out right alongside him, so close that we had to practically step on the bones of its outstretched hand to get over it. A scrap of cloth dangling from an overhanging branch brushed against my face as I stepped over the bones. I realized then that we must have been following the footsteps of many other mine victims, their accidents marking out a path of safety for those behind them.

It was the longest night of my life. At some point Yann slipped, twisting his ankle so that he had to limp.

He tried not to cry, but it must have hurt, and I heard his breathing come in short, choppy bursts. So I lifted him and carried him on my back. Boran, I knew, had his hands full helping Ma, who was so tired she had to be half hoisted, half dragged along. And still our guide kept moving on.

Then finally, the undergrowth of the jungle thinned, and we were on flat scrubland again, with only clumps of bushes dotting the landscape. In the distance, we heard voices. The guide crouched down low, and motioned for us to do the same. The voices approached, and Yann whimpered in fear. I could feel him trembling against me. I clamped my hand over his mouth, as we waited for the voices to pass.

And as they did, I listened to them talking, and found that I could not understand them. They were speaking Thai. A huge wave of relief flowed through me. We had made it out of Cambodia, and into Thailand.

Dawn brought with it our first glimpse of the border. A wasteland, it seemed at first sight — a vast barren plain, no fields, no trees, no shrubs, no houses. What had once been rice fields was now a mud plain, the earth tamped down as hard as rock by the hundreds of thousands of people walking over it. A few stands of shade trees dotted the plain, but many of these had already been chopped down for firewood, so that only a cluster of stumps were left. The countless tendrils of smoke from cooking fires of families camping everywhere meant that even the few trees left would soon be cut down for firewood.

As we made our way through this endless plain, it became more and more crowded. Whole families were sheltered under a flimsy piece of thatching, or under a piece of cloth stretched out between sticks. Everyone looked as thin and ragged as we were, swept together into haphazard piles like dried leaves against a fence.

So this was the border? Where were the mountains of free rice that we had heard rumors of? Where were the hospitals and schools that were supposed to have been built? Had we come all this way only to join this teeming crowd of refugees who were as poorly off as we were?

"Maybe we shouldn't have come," I said softly to Ma.

"Don't think like that," she said sharply. Then she managed a wan smile, and added, "You're tired, child. You'll feel better after some food."

What food? I wanted to ask, but held my tongue. The few provisions we had brought with us had long ago been eaten, and we had no jewelry, no money, nothing of value left to trade or buy anything with.

Just ahead of me, Uncle Kem had stopped, and was eyeing an empty spot at the edge of a tamarind tree. The area under the tree had already been staked out by families who had erected their makeshift campsites, but there was a spot partly dappled with shadow that looked unoccupied.

"How about right here?" he asked. I wasn't sure if he was asking for our opinion, or for the permission of the families already there. But since nobody said anything, he dropped the bundle of clothes he was carrying, and squatted down.

One by one, we did the same thing, in a rough semicircle around him. It was as good a place as any to call ours for now.

Within a matter of hours, it seemed, that bare patch of ground already had the feel of a home. Uncle Kem assigned each of us to simple tasks: Boran and Yann were to gather what branches and kindling they could cut, and bring it back. My cousin and I were to find water and bring a bucket of it back, and Mother would unpack our belongings. Uncle Kem himself went off to gather that most important of resources — information.

Soon we had built a little shelter of palmetto leaves and bare branches, which gave us some shelter from the sun. There was a full bucket of water, which I had drawn from a shallow well nearby, dug by people who had settled in before us. Mother had started a small camp-fire, and was setting a pot of water over it.

I peered into the pot hopefully. There was nothing in it but water. At least we'll have something warm to put in our stomachs, I thought — maybe there might even be a handful of leftover rice to make some gruel with. "Is there anything we can put in it?" I asked my mother. "Anything at all?"

Before she could reply, a girl from the campsite next to ours squatted down next to us and thrust something at me. "Here," she said, "put this in."

I looked at the big tin mug she held. It was brimming over with rice — not cooked rice, but rice grain. Once cooked, it would expand to three times that size — enough to feed our whole family. Mother came over and shook her head. "We have nothing to pay for it," she said.

The girl smiled, and poured the rice into our pot. Such full white grains they were, round and smooth like the first drops of monsoon rain, gleaming white in the dusk.

"Don't worry, aunt," the girl said. "You don't have to pay for this. We didn't, so why should you? We were given a fifty-kilo sack at the last distribution, so we've got more than enough for ourselves. There's so much rice here, even the mice are plump."

Ma was still shaking her head in disbelief, when Uncle Kem joined us. "It's true," he said. "They're giving out sacks of rice, and cooking oil and dried fish. And . . . and even fishnets, and hoe heads and . . ."

The girl nodded, then beckoned us to look behind the piece of cloth that served as a door for her shelter. "See? All this stuff? It's all been given to us."

Inside the thatching was a neat pile of supplies — a sack of milled rice, metal tools and rope, a plastic tarp, and even a shiny new bucket. My mother turned and flashed a big smile at me. "Still think we shouldn't have come, Nakri?" she said. I laughed with glee.

As our rice was simmering, Uncle Kem told us that the next distribution was scheduled to take place in another four or five days, and that all he needed to do was to register at some headquarters and get a card certifying that he was head of a household. "They don't give out everything at once," he said. "Sometimes it's fishnets, then another week it might be tools, or just rice . . ."

"JUST rice?" Yann echoed, incredulous. "Isn't rice all we need?"

And so it was — for a wonderful meal, anyway. That evening, sitting around the embers of the campfire, we ate until we were full. And not the quick, sloshy kind of fullness that comes from drinking soup or rice gruel, but the slow solid satisfaction that you get from food that needs to be chewed. I savored every mouthful, rolling the whole grains of rice under and around my tongue before chewing. It had been so long since we had had such smoothly polished, unbroken rice grains, that even without anything to go with it, the rice itself was a magnificent feast.

Within a few days, Uncle Kem had registered with the camp authority, and brought back supplies of our own — the same pieces of bright blue tarp our neighbors had, some rope, and rice. Rice! A big sack of it, each grain so whole and perfect. I ran my hands through the grains over and over, marveling at their texture and perfection — so unlike the broken gritty bits that we had grown used to.

Meanwhile, Yann had heard from the other kids about a place within a half-hour's walk, where every day workers ladled out bowls of stew for free, to every child who stood in line.

"At first they said only children who were five years old or less could get food there," Yann explained, "but then everyone just claimed to be five. Then they said only really skinny kids would be fed, and they had some funny way of measuring how tall we were, and how much we weighed, but that took so long that they gave up." Yann shrugged. "We're all skinny anyway, so I guess that's all right."

I went along with him for the first few times, to see what it was like, and to help him along because his twisted ankle was still hurting him.

And it was exactly as he had described it. A long scraggly line of young children were already waiting, when a truck roared into view, churning clouds of dust behind it. It ground to a stop sign that announced that this was Feeding Station Number Eight, and two burly men hoisted down a huge vat of food on their shoulder pole, walking carefully down a wooden gangplank from the truck. Four women started ladling the stew from the vat into the little bowl that each child held up, and the line started to move.

It all went quickly and quietly, with the children careful not to jostle each other lest they spill the precious food. The stew was still steaming hot, and smelled of coriander and pepper. When Yann had gotten his bowlful, I had a taste of it. There were chunks of squash and carrots in it, and even a shred of meat. I wished I were five years old, and could get my own bowl, but I took only a second spoonful, then handed it back to Yann, who was watching me hungrily. With that stew, and the rice Mother cooked, he would grow strong and plump in no time, I thought.

In the meanwhile, Uncle Kem had heard that there would be a distribution of rice seed coming up. "Imagine that — not just milled rice for eating," he told us over dinner one night, "but rice seed, for growing! With that, we can head home, and be back in time for the planting season."

His face was aglow with the light of the campfire embers, but also, I realized, by the hope that he could now resume life as he had always known it — as a rice farmer. He would go home to plough his fields, broadcast the rice seed, and watch them grow into tender green seedlings, then transplant the seedlings and tend them until they ripened into brown sheaves of rice, which he would harvest and thresh. Just like he had done every year of his life since he was born. And with the Khmer Rouge gone, he would have control over his own life again.

I could understand why he would feel so happy at the prospect, but I couldn't really share his joy. Home for me was not the village where he and my grandparents lived, but the city of Phnom Penh. Yet what was left of that life? A vision of its dark and deserted streets, overgrown with weeds, came to mind. How could it ever revert back to its gracious old self? Even if people drifted back to live in the city, and gradually opened up the shops and schools and offices, we wouldn't be able to go back to our old way of life, in our old home. Father was gone, and without him to support us, how would we be able to earn a living? And Teeda — how could I bear to live in the bedroom I had always shared with her, when she would never be there again?

I looked over at Mother, and I could see that her face was clouded with anxiety. Clearly, she was not as thrilled with the news of the rice seed distribution as her brother was. Still, when she saw me looking at her, she flashed me a reassuring smile. One step at a time, she seemed to be saying, little by little.

So I took her cue, and did not fret too much about what might happen next. Enough to know that we would have enough to eat for our next meal, especially when the food was as good as the free stew Yann was handed.

He looked forward to going to the feeding station every afternoon, half running, half hobbling on his sprained ankle. Ma worried that the sprain wasn't healing properly, and that he shouldn't be walking so far on it. But he begged to be allowed to go, and Ma grudgingly consented, but insisted that I go along as well, just to watch over him.

It was just as well that I did. One afternoon the food truck was late, so that the children in line were already hotter and hungrier than usual. Then, instead of ladling out stew from a big vat, the people in the truck started handing out a loaf of bread to each child. Stew you have to wait for, but bread you could snatch. A few of the bigger boys figured this out, and pandemonium broke out. Bread flew through the air, as some teenagers climbed up the sides of the truck to grab some for themselves, while others flung loaves out. There was a wild stampede for the bread as children got pushed aside, while men shoved their way toward the truck.

In the confusion, Yann tripped, and fell over with a sharp cry. Desperately, I tried to pull him loose, but his hurt leg was pinned under him, as people clamored over him trying to get closer to the truck. I crouched over him, shielding his head with my arms, trying to protect him.

Finally, gunshots rang out. Thai soldiers who patrolled the camp were firing their guns into the air, breaking up the crowd. The truck reversed, inching its way through the parting crowd, and drove away. Only after that did the crowd disperse.

I looked down at Yann. He was sobbing, whether from terror or pain, or both, I could not tell. His ankle was swollen, and there was a long gash up that leg.

I tried to pull him up, but he couldn't seem to support his own weight, much less walk. Blood was streaming down his leg, from the gash. When he saw that, his howls increased. Stifling my panic and trying to seem calm for his sake, I unwound Teeda's old scarf from my hair and wrapped it around his wound. That seemed to calm him down a little.

Looking around me for help, I saw a girl about my

own age straddling a baby brother on one hip. She looked vaguely familiar.

"Is he hurt bad?" she asked.

"I . . . don't know," I said shakily. At that, Yann started to sob again.

"You wait here. I'll go get your mother," the girl said.

I realized then who she was — the girl who had given us that mug of rice our first day here, and whose campsite was near ours.

"Thanks, I'll wait here," I told her.

As she ran off, her baby brother bouncing at her hip, she turned back and shouted at me, "My name's Jantu! What's yours?"

But she didn't wait for my reply before disappearing into the crowd.

By the time Jantu returned with Mother, Yann had fallen asleep, his head in the lap of my sarong.

"My poor baby!" Mother exclaimed.

Yann blinked. "I'm not a baby," he said.

While Mother was fussing over him, Jantu took charge. "There's a clinic at the western edge of the camp," she said. "They'll fix him up there."

"Where? How do we get there?" I asked.

Jantu looked surprised. "I'll show you, of course," she said.

And so we set off, with Mother carrying Yann in her arms. She had never been a strong woman, but she carried him without stopping or even slowing down, for mile after mile. I wanted to take my turn carrying him, but Ma only shook her head impatiently.

Walking behind her, I thought of the way she had cared for each of us as babies, feeding us, bathing us, watching over us day by day. How many thousands of days she has spent, trying to make sure we were safe. No wonder she was so fiercely protective of Yann now. I knew there was no way I could have pried him away from her at that point.

It was almost twilight by the time we approached the western edge of Nong Chan. There were tall watchtowers, manned by rifle-carrying Thai soldiers, who made sure the refugees couldn't slip farther into their country. Clustered under the watchtowers were some large sheds, nicely thatched but with no walls, which Jantu said served as the hospital wards for the wounded, or the malnourished, or the sick.

"Which one should we take Yann to?" Mother asked.

Jantu hesitated. "I'm not sure," she said. "I've . . . I've never been inside." She hung back, as if she had no intention of going in now either.

"Let's find out," Ma said firmly, and walked through the doorway of the nearest shed. Jantu reached out for my hand. I held onto it gladly, and we followed my mother.

In the dim light under the thatching, I could see rows of low cots, with people lying or sitting on them. It took my eyes a few seconds to adjust to the gloom, before I saw that each of these people had something missing: an arm, a leg, a hand, both legs. Where the arm or leg should have been, there was only a bandaged stump, soaked through with blood. Many of the people were moaning or tossing about restlessly.

Mother gasped, and backed out. I followed, pulling Jantu with me.

"Land mines," she said. "Lucky we didn't step on any."

The second shed was no better. Full of babies and toddlers so severely malnourished that even Yann looked robust compared with them. Some were being fed intravenously, and had plastic tubes of liquid strapped to their wrists. Others just lay there, eyes staring vacantly up at the ceiling. All of them had arms and legs so thin you could see the bones protruding under the loose skin. Ma stood riveted to one spot, staring at a baby so thin he looked like a plucked sparrow. Held gently in the arms of a wrinkled old woman who must have been his grandmother, he was suckling at her dry, flaccid breast.

"Why isn't he with his mother?" I asked Jantu quietly.

"She's probably dead," Jantu said. "At least he has someone. I've heard that one of the sheds is full of orphans. Stranded here with no family at all . . ."

I swallowed hard. What would it be like, I wondered, if I knew nobody, and nobody knew me?

It was not until we entered the third tent that someone offered to help us. A tall foreigner, a woman with red hair that frizzed out all over her head, stopped us and said something we couldn't understand.

Mother pointed at Yann's leg, and the foreign woman nodded, and gestured for him to be laid down on an empty cot. Ma sat down on it, but did not loosen her hold on Yann as the woman, a nurse, examined him.

More guttural words followed, accompanied by gestures. Through sign language, she communicated to us that she would clean Yann's wound, and set his ankle straight, by wrapping something tightly around it. Mother nodded her assent, and the nurse went to work on Yann.

And so Yann got his wound attended to, and after a day or two, he even seemed to enjoy being in the hospital. "You get two good meals a day here," he said, "and there's no waiting in line."

In between the meals, though, he would get bored and restless. I played games with him — paper, scissors, and rock, or guessing games. I showed him how to write the letters of the Cambodian alphabet, scratching each one out on the dirt floor with a stick. But what Yann loved most was being shown the photograph of our family that I had taken from our old house when Boran and I went back to Phnom Penh. It was worn thin by now, and the envelope was crinkled and streaked with dirt. Still, Yann would look at the faces in the photograph, and ask endless questions. How tall was Father? Why was Ma wearing those fancy shoes instead of slippers? What did I have in the schoolbag I was carrying?

If I didn't know the answers, I would make them up. And it didn't matter that my answers might vary from one day to the next. What Yann wanted was simply to be absorbed in a world outside of his immediate one.

As we were looking at the photograph on his cot one morning, the frizzy-haired nurse who had first tended Yann stopped, and looked at it too. "You?" she asked in

Khmer, pointing to Teeda. I felt a jab of satisfaction, that in the last five years, I must have grown up to look quite a bit like my sister.

"Me," I said, and pointed instead to the little girl standing next to Teeda.

The nurse smiled, then saw the envelope and picked it up. She frowned, then examined it with growing interest. Looking at me, she started talking excitedly, in her own language, gesturing at the letter. I had no idea what she was saying, so I only nodded dumbly.

She left, taking the envelope with her, and was soon back, with a Cambodian translator in tow. These hospital sheds, I had learned, always had at least three or four translators working in them, because the foreign doctors and nurses were from half a dozen different countries, and seemed to speak neither Khmer nor each other's languages.

"She's asking if the person who sent you this letter is a friend of yours," the translator told me.

I shook my head. "He knew my father," I said.

"And where's your father?"

I took a deep breath, but remained silent. My lips would not form that one word: dead. Somehow I felt that if I never said it, then it wouldn't be final.

The translator understood. He pushed his glasses up his nose, and said something to the nurse. Then he turned back to me. "She wants to know if you have tried writing him — the name on this return address?"

Together we looked at the envelope. The words were in English. Even if, once upon a time, I could have sounded out the words, I had forgotten how to read, much less write, in English. And besides, what would I say?

The woman seemed to have a very good idea of what she would say, though. "She wants to write a letter to him, for you," the translator said. "She wants to tell the sender of this letter, this friend of your father's, where you are now. She wants to ask him if he would help your family move to America."

This sounded so far-fetched that I laughed out loud. "Move to America?" I said. "Why not?"

"But she can't take our photo," Yann spoke up.

"That's right," I said. "She can take the envelope, but we're holding onto the photograph."

Later, I told Mother about this, wanting to share the joke with her, but she did not laugh. "America?" she echoed. "Your father always wanted to go there. Maybe this is his way of getting us there. Maybe he is still trying to take care of us. . . ." And she sat stroking Yann's hair, a faraway look in her eyes.

For a few days I wondered what would happen next. Every time I saw the frizzy-haired nurse, I would look at her expectantly, but since she never said anything about the letter, gradually I put it out of my mind altogether.

Staying with Yann in the hospital ward became a little boring. I started to explore the area around us, and saw that the shed next door was indeed full of orphans, or at least children who had been left to themselves. They were well fed and well cared for, but seemed listless, as if they didn't really care about anything much.

I brought Mother over to see them once, and she barely had time to sit down before she was surrounded by them, especially the littlest ones. She let them sit on her lap, and she would comb their hair, wash their faces, sing to them. Soon she was spending as much time over at the orphanage as she was with her own son.

Late one afternoon, I heard the sound of rhythmic clapping coming from the orphans' shed. I had been washing Teeda's old scarf, scrubbing the dirt and blood-stains off it with a bit of soap powder that the foreign nurse had given me. The homespun cloth had become so thin and threadbare from years of use that I had to be very careful not to rip it while washing it. Now, as I was wringing it dry, I saw that a small crowd of children was standing around a wooden table behind the orphanage, laughing and clapping.

Curious, I walked over and squirmed my way through the throng to the front. There, on the top of the table was a little girl, barely old enough to walk. Somebody had draped a garland of fresh white tuberoses on her, and she was playing with it, twirling it around her neck, waving her small arms up and lifting first one foot, then the other, all to the rhythm of the clapping. All by herself, having a wonderful time. She was dancing!

Soon another girl, about my age, started dancing too, her arched fingers circling so gracefully that I could tell at once that she must have been, at some point, trained as a dancer. The little girl on the table watched, trying to mimic the older one's gestures, much to everyone's delight. Someone brought out an oil barrel, and started drumming on it. Someone else had a homemade flute, carved out of a stick of bamboo, and was playing that.

As the dancing continued, a few other girls joined in, shy and giggling, not actually dancing, but swaying their waists and moving their arms to the music. Gradually they were steered into two, then three rows, the taller and more adept ones in front, the younger ones behind them. Someone was moving between the rows, guiding their movements, straightening one girl's shoulder, lifting another one's chin. I realized with a start that it was my mother. She had become their dance teacher.

She caught my eye, and beckoned for me to come up and join them. I recoiled.

No, Ma, I wanted to shout. Don't teach them. You're our teacher, mine and Teeda's!

A vivid image flashed through my mind, of my sister dancing in the palace pavilion, her graceful arms being adjusted by our mother as I watched. Mother and daughter had almost been reflections of each other, their faces filled with the same strong determination. Something was being passed from one to the other, I had realized then, something more than just the art of dancing. It had to do with love, and beauty, and a fierce commitment to continuity.

Teeda was gone, and now Mother was trying to pass that same spirit to someone else, to these strangers who had never even danced before. How could she?

I turned away, blinking back tears. In my hands was Teeda's scarf, still damp from the washing.

Suddenly I wanted Teeda back. So much. I wanted to

be near her, to touch her, to watch her dance in front of me as I learned how to move from the way she moved. I wrapped her old scarf around my hair, draping it low across my eyes to hide my tears, and ran off.

Barely ten steps later, I collided with someone. Wiping my eyes hastily with the damp scarf, I looked up and saw the frizzy-haired nurse. She must have been waiting for me, because she was holding out Father's old envelope and gesturing excitedly. As she pushed the envelope into my hands, I understood only one word: "America!"

Soon the translator came up to us, beaming. "Yes, America!" he echoed. "Your father's friend wrote back. He's arranging it all. You can go to America!"

"I don't want to go to America," I blurted out. "I just . . . I just want to go home!" I flung away the old envelope, and the hot tears that I had been holding back streamed down my face. I felt further away from Teeda than ever.

Someone must have picked up the envelope, of course, because a few nights later, it became the focus of attention back at our family campsite. Yann had been discharged from the clinic the day before, and was now resting comfortably under the blue tarp that served as our makeshift home.

"What exactly did the foreign nurse say?" Boran asked, for the third time.

And so I was made to tell the whole story over, explaining that this foreign colleague of our father had gotten his church group to find a family who would sponsor us. "That means they will see that we get properly settled in America," I said. "But just us, Father's immediate family . . ."

I glanced over uneasily at Uncle Kem, unsure of how he would take this.

"I wouldn't have gone anyway," Uncle Kem said gruffly. "My place is back home, now that I have enough seed to plant next year's rice." He nodded at the bags of seed rice that Yann was using as a pillow. "Besides, I want to go back and take care of my mother. She'll still be at home."

Home? Where was my home? Not Grandma's and Uncle Kem's village, really. Much as I liked it, I had always just been a visitor there. And certainly not that broken-down, deserted house my brother and I went back to in Phnom Penh — it could never feel like home again, without Father and Teeda living with us.

Could America ever become home for me? Even the moon would be more familiar, I thought. The moon at least I could see. But America I couldn't even begin to imagine.

The envelope had come from America. I watched it being passed from hand to hand around the campfire, until it was given back to me. I held it close to the flames and examined it. Not the stamp, not the card inside, not even the family photo — but the little corner where the address of Father's friend was written in English.

I remembered the sounds that foreign nurse had made when she had read out the return address, and I studied the unfamiliar shapes of the letters, and sounded them out now: "Fill-a-dal-fia," I read out softly. Then two more letters, "Pa." Was that going to be my new home, then? Was there somewhere in America called "Pa"? I said it aloud, "Pa," and it sounded like I was calling out for my father.

Then I felt something very strange. I felt my father's presence, as if he had heard my call and responded by coming into our midst. I stroked the envelope, and realized it was a direct connection with my father, almost as if he had personally passed it to me as a gift. And indeed it was, because with that letter he had given us a link to the outside world, and a start to a whole new life.

Part Four

*O*nce the process was set in motion, everything happened quite quickly and efficiently, as if we were water scooped up in a waterwheel and carried along rung after rung. From the sprawling fields of Nong Chan, to the barbed wire enclosure of Khao I Dang, to the new holding center of Panat Nikom, we were shunted from one refugee camp to another, each one more organized than the one before. Along the way we submitted to medical checkups, learned how to apply for sponsorship, and were questioned and cross-questioned in long interviews.

During the interview, the official — sitting behind a long, wooden desk just like the Khmer Rouge cadres we encountered after we were evacuated from Phnom

Pehn — looked us over and asked Ma, "How many children do you have?"

"Four," Ma said.

"Sons or daughters?"

"Two sons, and two daughters," Ma said nervously.

The official raised an eyebrow. "I see your two sons, but . . ." — he made a show of peering behind me — "only one girl."

Ma bit her lip.

"Where is your other daughter?"

Ma swallowed hard. "She . . . she's not here, sir."

"Where is she?"

"She . . ." Ma could not get the word out. Twisting at the ends of Teeda's black scarf, I tried to speak for her, but found that my throat had constricted.

"Well?"

Finally Boran spoke. "She's dead, sir. She died two years ago."

"Fine," the man said brusquely. "I guess she won't be going with you."

I felt as if I was abandoning Teeda then, leaving her so far behind that there would be no way for her ever to catch up with us again. I don't want to go either, I almost blurted out. But Boran gave me a sharp look, and

142

so I just kept twisting my sister's old scarf and kept quiet.

That had been the last step, the last hurdle in the obstacle course before we were cleared to leave for America.

A few weeks after that, we were ushered onto a bus, and driven through the streets of bustling Bangkok, to the airport on its outskirts.

I had no idea what flying would feel like, and thought of the way hawks and sparrows flew, swooping and darting in smooth arcs in the sky, or the way kites flew, jerked sharply upward by each tug of the string until they hung suspended in space. Or even of the feel of flying on playground swings when I was little, the wind slashing back and forth against me.

But jet planes, I discovered, did not fly like that. The jet moved the way a huge truck would move, with grim, self-contained energy. It charged down the long runway, gaining so much momentum that the whole cabin shook with it. Then suddenly, without warning, it jutted sharply upward, and we were all pushed back into our seats, as if an invisible hand forced us backward. Beside me, I could hear my mother utter a quick prayer to Buddha.

I leaned forward and looked out the window. The

ground was receding rapidly under us, but I didn't feel as if I was flying over it. The airport buildings, the palm trees and canals, the highways choked with buses and cars, the dense cluster of buildings — all slid below me, as if being sucked backward, faster and smaller every passing second. If anything, it felt like a form of dying, not flying. Maybe this is what death is like, when our souls leave our bodies, I thought. Exhilarated and frightened at the same time. Was this what Teeda felt when she died? I pulled her old scarf more tightly around my neck, glad for its familiar feel.

Soon, the city of Bangkok was left behind, and green fields, square patches in varying shades of green, slid into view beneath us. The Chao Phraya River, a glittery ribbon, twisted and turned among them. I saw a spot of bright orange, and realized it was the top of a temple roof.

"Look, a temple!" I said, tugging at my mother's sleeve. Quickly, she leaned over me and gazed down.

"So small!" she breathed, awestruck. Then, with deep reverence, she put her palms together and bowed her head over them, as the speck of orange roof slid under us.

And then there was only the sea. Flat and blue and endless, so far below us that you couldn't see any ships, let alone waves. The Pacific Ocean: I remembered a map of Cambodia in a geography textbook I had, in my "other life" in Phnom Penh. The closest I had ever gotten to the ocean was to watch the muddy water of the Mekong River flowing along the promenade near the palace — and that water would have to pass through Vietnam and a web of deltas before reaching the sea. And now I was flying over it, without once ever having even touched it.

Then, even the blue ocean was lost to view, as we skimmed through a white layer of clouds. They were so thick I felt I could roll and squeeze a handful of it into a tight ball like the dough inside of the French bread sold in the Central Market, and eat it. But the jet plane just pierced right through, and soared into an overturned bowl of liquid gold. It was the setting sun, so close that I felt I could throw a stone at it. And the colors! Splashes of red and gold tinted the clouds, turning them into rolling, glowing fields of soft fire. If only Grandma's loom was threaded with silken threads of such sunset colors, I thought, what an incredible sarong she would weave!

But where was Grandma? And where was Phnom Penh, and the garden behind our old house? Where were the fields in the work camp in Phum Thmei where we worked, and the thatched shed where we slept? Where was the vast dry terrain of the refugee camps on the border, with its thousands of oxcarts? Somewhere — down there, below the glowing clouds, I knew they were still there. But it seemed as if they were of another world, another time, left far, far below and behind.

I looked out the window for a long time, watching the sunset colors gradually fading into gray and then black. I spread Teeda's checkered scarf over my shoulders, and as I snuggled into its familiar texture and smell, I grew drowsy and fell asleep.

In my dreams I saw Teeda, dressed again in her apsara costume, gracefully dancing the dance of the angels, lifting her left foot arched flat up toward the sky in the classical gesture of flying through the heavens. I called to her, and she heard me, and beckoned for me to join her, her long fingers curved far back. I arched my foot like her, and I was flying too, after her, floating on a sea of glowing clouds. Is this Heaven then? I asked her. Is this where we are now?

She smiled, and then my arm was being grasped, hard. Someone was shaking me, smiling at me, the smile like Teeda's but not quite. "Are we there?" I mumbled. "In paradise?"

"Not quite, but close," Boran said, his smile broad. "We're landing in America!"

America was not like any paradise I had ever imagined at all. I had never felt such absolute cold. Like gigantic razor blades, the cold wind scraped against my skin, chilling me to my very bones. As soon as we stepped out of the plane, I wrapped the checkered shawl tight around my shoulders, but it didn't do any good. There were clumps of white on the ground, lying inert and hard. I knew it was snow, and I had wanted for a long time to see some, but now that I had, I didn't like the look of it. Like dead clouds that had fallen out of the heavens. My bare toes, jutting out of rubber sandals, touched some, and I didn't like the feel of it either.

Luckily, we didn't have to be in the cold and dark for very long — just a few feet from the bottom of the stairs was a big bus, all lit up with neon lights like a modern department store. I was one of the last ones to get on before the bus, now filled with passengers, closed its doors. As we drove away, I craned my neck for one last look at the jet that we were just in — our last link with our old lives — and soon it too disappeared in the darkness.

Then there was a blur of bright lights and huge rooms, with us standing in long lines hearing an endless stream of strange words over an intercom system, everything so orderly and so clean it seemed unreal. There was no hint of any natural world outside of this — not a streak of mud or a simple growing plant of any kind.

The four of us, Mother, Boran, Yann, and I, were treated as one unit. Our papers were processed together, and we were ushered through the lines together. Finally, following dozens of other Cambodians from our plane, we walked out some doors that swung wide open by themselves. Before us stood a crowd of noisy, huge, pale-faced giants — Americans! If they had been growling tigers, they couldn't have been more frightening. There were so many of them, and they all looked so strange. I had to resist the urge to turn right around and go back through the doors.

But little Yann was already running ahead. "Look!" he said, pointing over at a particularly large American. "He's holding a sign in Khmer!"

"Sokha," Boran read. "Could that be for us?"

"Must be," Yann said. And fearlessly he walked up to him, and tugged at the sign carrier's shirtsleeve. "Me Sokha!" he shouted. "Me! I'm Yann Sokha."

The giant, who had a bushy brown beard, peered down at Yann. "Sokha?" he repeated.

Yann nodded vigorously.

The bushy beard parted, and the mouth inside split into a wide, bushy smile. It was incredible the way the thick hair on either side of this man's mouth stretched apart, revealing a row of white teeth. He said something that we didn't understand, but there was one word we all heard: "Sokha."

Yann gestured to us, and announced, "Sokha. We are the Sokha family."

"*Sok sabai chea tay?*" the woman next to the bearded giant said. She was big too, and had bright-yellow hair, but a friendly voice. And a normal, nonhairy smile.

"You speak Khmer?" Ma said, delighted.

But the woman replied in English. It was soon apparent that "How are you?" was the one Khmer sentence she had learned. But it was enough to make us warm up to her. Soon we were all smiling and nodding at each other.

"Anna," the woman said, pointing to herself. "Sam," she said, pointing to the beard.

So we took turns to say our own names too, and soon we were shaking hands all around. Yann became our spokesman. "Hello," he kept saying. "Good-bye. Hello, good-bye."

They led us over to a quieter corner, and pulled open a big backpack they had brought with them. Inside were enough socks and shoes, woolen hats, gloves, and scarves for us all. From another bag, the man brought out four coats, one for each of us. Everything was too big, except for the clothing for Yann. Maybe American children, at least, were the same size as Khmer ones.

Still, it felt good to be under something so thick and heavy when we were led out into the cold again. This time it was a longer walk, across several lanes busy with traffic, and then into a dark, many-storied building with low walls, where cars were parked in neat rows, stacked one floor over another. I had no idea how, with so many hundreds of cars together, our hosts found theirs, but they did.

It was a blue van, with three rows of seats inside. The middle door slid open, and the four of us climbed into it, behind our hosts. A switch of the ignition, a turn of the wheel, and we were driving in dizzying circles down, down, down a circular ramp until, finally, we cleared the building, and were on solid American ground.

The drive took over an hour, but I couldn't make out much of the countryside that we were driving through since it was pitch dark. All I saw were two lanes of headlights and taillights whizzing past. Then we turned off the big highway and slowed down, driving down quieter, narrower streets until we finally arrived at a big, two-storied white house.

House? No, it was a palace.

Not like the airy pavilions inside the palace compound where Teeda and I used to dance, but a palace just the same. I had seen pictures in magazines years ago, when we lived in Phnom Penh, of the way Americans lived. And vaguely I remembered a few movies where we saw the insides of their homes — but none of that prepared me for the modern magic of this house.

We had barely stepped inside their front door when, with a flip of the switch, Anna turned on the lights. Blinking back the bright light that suddenly flooded the room, I looked around me. There was an array of sofas and chairs, paintings on the walls, shelves lined with books, and underneath it all a plush white carpet, so soft that I could feel my feet sinking into it.

Anna said something that evidently meant a welcome, as she stepped into the room and beckoned us in. My mother was in front of me, and I could sense her hesitation. She glanced down at her shoes, and I understood why.

"She hasn't taken hers off," I whispered to my mother.

"Yes, but . . . ," but how could we step onto this soft carpet with shoes on? Awkwardly my mother bent down and slipped her shoes off. Boran and I and Yann nudged ours off as well.

Anna was making protesting sounds, but her husband said something that cut her off midsentence. I saw them exchange a quick glance. Then Anna bent over and took her own shoes off, and behind us I noticed Sam doing the same thing. Quietly, they followed our example, and lined their shoes up neatly in a row next to ours. I decided that I liked them.

"Hungry?" Sam said to Yann with his hairy smile, rubbing his round belly. Yann picked up on the meaning of the word fast. "Hungry!" he echoed, rubbing his own stomach. Sam laughed.

He led us to an adjoining room, not carpeted this time, but just as clean and bright and new. There was a long wooden table in the middle of it, surrounded by six chairs, with a plate, a glass, and silverware arranged before each one. If King Sihanouk was coming for dinner, I thought, the table couldn't have looked more elegant.

While Anna and Sam busied themselves with pots and pans, we stood around awkwardly, not knowing quite what to do. Yann wandered over to the sofa and picked up a book lying on it.

"Don't touch!" Mother scolded.

But Yann ignored her. "Look!" he said, and held it up. On the cover was a photograph, in color, of two Khmer dancers in full costumes, complete with golden head-dresses. We crowded around Yann as he turned the pages. It was full of photos of Cambodia, of water buffaloes and green rice fields, markets teeming with baskets of mangoes and papayas and rambutan and other fresh fruits, and, of course, of Angkor Wat temple, with its stone carvings and huge stupas. Everything looked so familiar, and yet so strange, because the peaceful, happy scenes were like nothing we had seen for many, many years. Yann could not even remember ever having seen them, because he asked, in a small awed voice, "Is this Cambodia?"

Mother nodded. "Before the war," she said softly.

"So do they . . ." Yann glanced over at our hosts, "do they think this is what it was like, where we came from?"

Images of the desolate landscape where refugees like us lived under bits of plastic tarp, of stick-thin farmers in black uniforms being marched out to dig ditches in the fields, of abandoned schools and desecrated temples, of maimed boys and starving babies, all this flashed through my mind. How could someone like our gentle hosts — who lived within the safety of this beautiful home — ever know what the real Cambodia was like now?

I didn't know how to answer Yann. Quietly, Mother took the book from him and closed it.

Then Sam was calling out to us, beckoning us over to the dining table. Platters heaped high with food had been set in the middle of it, more food than I had ever seen at any one time in my life. Not even during the temple festivals, when we offered food to the monks, had I seen such a lavish spread. There was roast chicken and curry and stir-fried vegetables and shrimp and noodles and a big bowl of white rice. My mouth watered, and I had to swallow hard.

"Sit, sit," Sam said, gesturing for us to sit down. "Anywhere."

"Sit," Yann echoed softly. "Anywhere." At this rate, he was going to be speaking English in no time, I thought.

Anna and Sam sat at either end of the long table, and we seated ourselves on either side of it. They clasped their hands together, and bowed their heads. Yann immediately did the same thing, so we all did too.

Sam murmured something, which sounded rather like a monk starting up a chant, but he didn't get very far before he lifted his head and beamed around at us. "Eat," he said.

Yann approved. "Eat!" he said.

Soon our plates were piled high with food, with Anna busy ladling things out because we didn't want to seem greedy by helping ourselves. It was so tasty — all the rich flavors of cilantro and coriander, of anise and lemongrass, of coconut cream and curry, that I had not tasted for years, now burst like fireworks in my mouth. But surely this wasn't American cooking? We had been told they ate big slabs of meat, bland and unseasoned.

"You make?" Yann asked, between mouthfuls of chicken.

They laughed, and at first I thought they were laughing at his poor English, but Anna shook her head, and pointed vaguely out the window. "Restaurant," she said, "a Thai restaurant. You like it?"

"Like it," Yann echoed.

There wasn't much other conversation. We traded names again, to make sure we had gotten each other's right, then Yann traded them the English and Khmer words for things like rice, chicken, water, curry, while the rest of us kept rather quiet.

Incredible as it may seem, we ate as much as we could possibly eat and still there was so much left over. I felt uncomfortably full, as if the skin on my stomach was stretched too tight. And still our hosts were pressing us to eat more.

My mother shook her head. "Thank you, but we've eaten too much already," she said politely, in Khmer. "And besides, we should save some for tomorrow."

They must have understood at least the gist of what she meant, because they got up, and started to clear the table, stacking the various plates on top of each other. I looked around, half expecting servants to come help. It seemed strange that people as wealthy as Sam and Anna, who could provide such a feast, had no servants to help them clean up afterward.

"We must help," Ma said.

So we got up as well, and brought our plates over to a counter in the kitchen. Sam was behind the counter, scraping the leftover chicken and vegetables off the plates. Curiously, I peered over at what he was scraping the food into, expecting to see a bucket, perhaps, or a bowl. Instead it was a square metal bin, whose lid he somehow kept propped up by pushing a pedal at the base of the bin. He lifted his foot from the pedal, and the lid dropped down. So this was where they stored leftover food? Boran was next to me, also curious, and together we stepped up to take a closer look. When Sam had moved off to gather more dirty plates, Boran went up to the bin and pushed the pedal. The lid jerked up.

Boran gasped. For a long moment he stared at the food bin. Then, abruptly, he turned and walked away.

"Boran, what is it?" I asked. I saw his shoulders shaking, and I thought he was laughing. But what could be so funny about that food bin?

Sam came back, and started scraping more food into the bin. But not just food — the paper napkins that we had used, a plastic bag, an empty can — they were all dropped into the open bin. All that food, I realized — they weren't saving it, they were throwing it out! The bin was for garbage.

And I understood then why my brother's shoulder had been shaking like that. Boran was doing something I had never in my life seen him do — not when our father was taken away from us, not when our sister died, not when he was tied to that stake for three days and three nights: Boran, my big brother, was sobbing.

I should have felt happy with this new life, but there was an air of unreality to it all, as if my eyes were floating above me, and watching me go through the motions of living hero. The visible, functional part of me was busy learning and adjusting to this new world. How to work all the buttons and dials and switches in the house, how to run one machine for washing clothes, another for washing dishes, yet another for sucking up the dirt from the carpet. There were so many new things to learn, and I was intrigued by them all.

And yet, there was always another, totally separate part of me that kept to myself, and wanted nothing to do with this place and instead missed the familiar texture and smells of Cambodia. I remembered those mine victims in the Nong Chan hospital, with their arms or legs sawn off, and thought how I now understood a bit of how they felt. Except that instead of a missing limb, I was missing my entire head, with its storage of rich memories.

We tried to be helpful in the household, but didn't know quite what to do. Anna and Sam never made us feel as if we were in the way, but after a few days of living at their home, we felt as if we were imposing on them too much. How much longer would it be before we might be able to move out into our own place? The re-settlement teachers at Khao I Dang camp had told us we would have a home of our own, provided for by the government. When would we get assigned to ours? I wanted to ask Anna, but didn't know how to do it without seeming rude. Besides, although my English was improving, it was still too rudimentary to carry on much of a conversation.

Without being prompted, however, Anna told us the answer. "It's all arranged with public housing," she announced one morning. "They've assigned you a nice apartment nearby. Three bedrooms, two bathrooms," she said. "Want to go look at your new home?"

Within moments, we had packed what little we had, and were dressed and waiting for her by the front door, our various bags and packages at our feet.

And so we moved into Apartment 217 G, on Pleasant

Street, next to Public School 76. There were indeed three bedrooms, just as Anna had said, but there was also a kitchen, a dining room, a living room, and two bathrooms. We wandered back and forth through the empty rooms, as if by walking in them enough times, we might fill them up a little. "Why do we need so many rooms?" Mother asked, a worried look on her face. "What are we going to do with them all?"

I didn't really care. What mattered to me was that I now had a room of my own. I could go into it, close the door behind me, and I would be all alone. I did this that first afternoon we were there, and it felt . . . so peaceful. That empty space with four walls was all mine, and as I closed my eyes and breathed, in and out, in and out, I felt as if I could gradually expand into the space, my own space. I could feel my whole being relaxing into solitude.

The other rooms filled up soon enough. Anna took us to places that sold used furniture and clothes, and anything we could possibly need. Even by Khmer standards, these things were not expensive, and we soon bought enough to make the empty rooms feel homey: four mattresses, a table and four chairs, an armchair, two lamps, pots and pans, and eight plates and eight cups. (At first we picked out only four plates and four cups, but then Mother got extravagant and said: "Let's get a spare set!" So we did.) We also picked out pieces of clothing for ourselves — jeans and sweaters and shirts and even a towel each. Anna kept taking more clothes off the racks to give us, but Mother politely rejected them, not just because she didn't want Anna to spend so much on us, but simply because she didn't see the need for them.

As if that wasn't enough, we were then taken to another store, an absolutely huge place called, appropriately enough, a "Super-Market."

As soon as we stepped inside, I understood why Americans threw out their leftover food. They could just go to a supermarket and get more. Huge slabs of meat behind glass, or wrapped up in clear plastic; mounds of fresh fruits and vegetables, which were moistened by jets of spray; shelves of bread and cakes; and these were only the things I recognized. There were long aisles of cans, boxes, bottles of food and drink whose contents I could only guess at.

People wandered around, taking whatever they wanted from the shelves and putting it into these wire carts. Yann's jaw dropped as he watched them.

"You take what you want?" he asked Anna.

She smiled. "Well, you have to pay for it, of course!"

But it didn't seem that paying would be a problem for any of these shoppers. They piled their wagons high, almost carelessly tossing things in — without examining or squeezing them, without comparing prices, and of course without bargaining or haggling, since there was nobody to do that with.

In front of us was a very fat woman, shambling behind a cart stacked high with food. "Think you'll get to be like her soon, Ma?" Boran teased. Mother reached out and slapped him lightly on the back, and smiled. My throat tightened — I hadn't seen Mother being playful for such a long time!

We wandered all over the store, and took a long time picking out what to put into our cart: toothbrushes, toothpaste, toilet paper, soap. And, of course, food. A whole chicken, plucked clean and encased in plastic; onions, carrots, scallions, and cabbage; bananas and oranges; a dozen eggs, each one neatly slotted into its own hole in a cardboard carton; a loaf of bread already sliced up; and a small bag of white rice. Again, Anna kept trying to put more things into our cart, but Mother kept shaking her head. Too much, too fast. I think we all felt overwhelmed.

Anna probably realized this, because after a while she went quiet, and didn't object when we indicated that we had bought enough, even though our cart was only half filled.

It was a proud moment when, after she had dropped us off at our apartment building, Mother unlocked the front door with her key, and we each carried a brown paper bag full of food into our new home. We stood around the refrigerator as Mother unpacked the bags and carefully placed each item of food inside. When she was done, she stood aside and took a deep breath.

"There," she said, beckoning us to come closer.

We looked inside, my brothers and I. On the first shelf was the chicken and the loaf of bread. Below that were the vegetables and oranges. On the bottom shelf was the carton of eggs. Yann started clapping in delight, his little hands making a series of light noises in the empty apartment. I closed the refrigerator door and hugged him hard. We were home.

It seemed like we hardly had time to get used to our new home before Anna was preparing us for yet another major change. "School," she announced firmly, pointing out the window of our apartment.

Across the field from our apartment building was a set of redbrick buildings, their windows glinting in the sun. For some days now my brothers and I had kept a keen watch over it. We had seen the doors of that building swung open at the sound of a buzzer, and out would fly swarms of children, shouting and laughing and running, their heads swathed in bright woolen hats and scarves against the winter cold. Like birds released from those crowded cages near the temples back home, they would scatter out into the open.

"Our school?" Yann asked Anna, his voice hopeful and scared at the same time.

"Your school," Anna said emphatically. "And over there, next to it, Nakri and Boran's school too. You're all going to study there."

"Study?" Yann echoed, wide-eyed.

I glanced over at my little brother. Barely a toddler when the Khmer Rouge took over Phnom Penh, he had never been inside a school in his life.

I tried to remember my own school days, sitting in a neat row in front of a blackboard, a newly sharpened pencil in my hand. How long ago that seemed now. I was not sure that I would be comfortable inside a classroom anymore, especially one in this strange foreign land.

"Must go?" I asked shyly, in English.

Anna nodded. "Now," she said, reaching out for Yann's hand.

One by one, she took us to the office of the school that we were to go to, and sat through the interviews with the administrators to have us enrolled. Yann was to be in first grade, I would start at eighth, and Boran would be in high school, in eleventh grade.

My brothers and I compared notes on it afterward, and we realized that we had each gone through a similar process. We were told not to be upset if at first we couldn't understand what was being taught in the classes — that was only natural and to be expected, because English was not our "first language." We would each attend special classes in English as a Second Language — ESL for short — and slowly but surely we would catch up with our classmates.

"A lot of children from countries like Mexico and China and Russia have done the same thing in our schools," Anna said. By the end of their first or second year, she claimed, they were usually fluent in English, and would get even better grades than their American classmates!

I shook my head in disbelief.

"But, yes, it happens," Anna said. "You just have to try hard — very hard."

"Not me," Boran said in Khmer. "I'm too old. I can't learn another language. I won't."

I worried about his attitude, but there was nothing I could do to change it.

Besides, I was too busy calming my own fears about starting school. I was going to try my hardest to learn, to adapt, to be a good American student, but suppose I couldn't? In the privacy of my own bedroom, I would lie on my mattress and take deep breaths, preparing myself for the ordeal that lay ahead.

It was even worse than I had expected. I felt as if I had been tossed into the middle of a stormy sea with shackles on and left to drown. I was overwhelmed, and felt as if I was already deep under water, where the sounds and shapes around me were all blurry. Nothing made any sense — not the words people uttered at me, nor the looks they gave me, nor the gestures they made toward me. Nobody stayed still. In class they all moved about, and talked back to the teacher, and laughed among themselves. Then the buzzer would sound and everyone would explode out of their chairs and rush around a maze of corridors until they had found seats in another classroom. Again and again, it would happen, until I lost count of how many times I moved, swept up and engulfed by the crowd, into yet another class. Somehow, someone always seemed to lead me along to the next room, but it wasn't always the same person — and I had no idea what classroom I was in, or what was being taught. Breathe, I told myself. Hang on tight, and breathe — soon the day will be over and you can go into your room, and close the door.

There, I would take off my socks and shoes and peel off those stiff jeans that still, after all these weeks, felt strange to me. Wrapping a sarong and draping Teeda's old scarf loosely around my neck, I would curl up in bed, and gaze for hours at the patch of sky outside the bedroom window as the pale winter light faded. I did not study, because I didn't even know how to start. And I did not even think, because thinking was all tied up in remembering, and memories only dragged me deeper into the dark murky hole that I could feel myself sinking into. I would just lie there and hope that enough of the panic and dread would drain away, that I could get up the next morning and get through another day.

Then, in the middle of a particularly awful day, I passed by a classroom from which strange sounds were coming. Music — not the classical music of Khmer xylophones or pipes, but music nevertheless. I stopped short, and listened. The notes had a rhythm and pattern to them that I intuitively understood. Long and sweet, mellow, like water flowing in a clear stream. I stood by the doorway and could not move. Someone — was it the teacher? — gently led me inside and motioned me into a seat. I sat there, and did not have to remember to breathe deep or look straight ahead. I could just lose myself and listen, because finally, I was hearing something that made sense to me.

I had no idea how it was arranged, but soon I had dropped one class (I think it was about American history, but I'm not sure) and was allowed to take a music class in its place. I was asked to choose an instrument, but everything looked so strange and metallic that I didn't dare touch anything. Then I saw a long, smooth flute, not so different from the flutes we had at home, and which I had learned to play at my grandmother's house. Teeda had danced to its music as I played it. This flute was made of wood instead of bamboo, but it had similar holes drilled into it. I picked it up, placed my fingers over the holes, blew out experimentally, and was thrilled at the sweet clear notes that came out.

"This one," I said to the music teacher.

He smiled. "Seems like you already know how to play it," he said.

I nodded. "I play it before, at home," I said carefully. And smiled. It was the first time I had spoken a complete sentence in English. The flute had helped me find my voice.

In the next few weeks, I learned how to play the scales, up and down — the sequence of notes clear and logical, but unlike our half tones at home. I also learned how to read music. It was so much easier than reading English and memorizing the long list of vocabulary words! Each note corresponded to a mark made on specially lined sheets, and I soon learned how to play the notes indicated by the mark. All those mornings that I had spent in dance class in the pavilion, watching the musicians in their starched white shirts tapping out the musical notes on bamboo slats, even playing with the instruments afterward, learning to sound out simple melodies — all that was like a reservoir of knowledge and experience that I could now tap into. It wasn't that different from playing the flute at home, and it came very naturally to me. Best of all, when I played my notes, they merged with the other notes played by the other students in the class, so that it felt as if we were all talking together, in the same language.

I was allowed, encouraged even, to take the flute home with me to practice.

And so I did, but I didn't close my door anymore. Sitting on my mattress, my back leaning against the wall, I would play the melodies on the music sheets in front of me, taking delight that I was really learning a new language.

Gradually, I learned my way around the school too. The classrooms and corridors became less of a maze, and I could find my way from one class to another, and to my locker, without somebody having to guide me. At first, I was very aware of how different everyone looked, with their pale skin and water-pale eyes, but after a while, I became so used to it that sometimes I would see my own face reflected from a mirror in the crowd, and think: Who is that dark girl over there? It was a very strange feeling, to be startled by what you look like, who you are.

Without realizing it, I was deliberately avoiding making eye contact with anyone, careful to keep my gaze always in the middle distance. Once in a while, I would catch someone smiling or waving, but I wouldn't be sure if it was meant for me, and I didn't want to chance finding out that it might not be. So I kept to myself, walked by myself, ate by myself. It was not hard to do. In fact, it wasn't that different from being in the work camps back in Cambodia, where I was always on guard, and careful not to attract attention. The less people noticed me, the less trouble I would have to face. Just like it had been with Hawk Eye.

Unlike me, Yann loved school. He blossomed, unfolding as quickly as a water lily in the morning light. At dinner he would chatter nonstop, his Khmer already mixed with English, as he talked about his new friends, the new games he had learned to play, the new cartoon characters on TV. Ma would listen, proud and loving, as he burbled on. But then Ma was proud and loving no matter what we did. It was enough for her that we had enough to eat and a safe place to sleep — after so many years of living in fear and uncertainty, that was all it took to make her happy.

Boran did not have it as easy as Yann. In fact, he must have hated classes even more than I did, because after two months he announced that he had found a job at a gas station, and was quitting school. Ma protested, but only weakly, because she could tell when Boran was determined. He was learning nothing at school, he insisted, and staying on would only be a waste of time. What he did not say, but which I understood, was how demeaning and lonely it was to wander around like a ghost among teenagers who seemed so brash and supremely confident in themselves.

Boran said his job would earn him over a hundred and fifty dollars a week, which seemed like an impossibly high salary to us, plus he would be learning something useful on the side. At the gas station, he would at first just be manning the pumps ("I only have to understand three words: Super, Regular, and Unleaded," he said), but he would also apprentice with the mechanics there, and take a night course on it as well. He could be an auto mechanic in less than a year, he claimed, and then he could earn twice, three times what he could now. "I know what I'm doing, Ma," he said. What he meant was: Don't tell me what to do — you don't know how things work here. Ma understood the implied putdown in his tone, and kept quiet.

I was the only one who felt a nagging sense of discontent, and because I didn't want to burden my family with it, I kept my frustration pretty much to myself, even at home. The winter months dragged on, grim and gray and cold, and the ground beneath my boots was frozen as hard as concrete. Like the ground, I felt as if something inside me had become cold and hard too.

It was only in the solitude of my own room, when I was playing the flute, that I would express some of what I felt. A loneliness, certainly, but worse than that — a feeling that something had broken inside me, and that there was nothing I could do to put the broken bits back together. Aside from my own small family, I had lost touch with everything I had ever known in my previous, pre-American life. The familiar sounds and sights and smells that had swirled around me in Cambodia, all that had disappeared. Where had it gone? Had it been real at all? What had replaced it? It seemed as if I had lived in one world before and I was living in another one now. The two worlds were so separate that there seemed no connection between the two. Was it still the same me? How could it be?

So often, I wanted to talk to Teeda. I missed her. With her I could have shared what I was going through, knowing that she would be feeling something similar too. And with her, I would have had somebody to look up to, so that I would know what to do next, instead of always feeling lost, always having to grope my way through blindly.

"Grope." "Cope." I had learned the two English words during the same lesson, and they were always linked in my mind. I coped by groping. For almost half my life, ever since I was ejected out of a sheltered childhood in Phnom Penh, I had had to cope. I learned how to cope, by taking small, cautious steps, one at a time, hands extended to help me feel my way, groping, always groping my way along.

And so I continued to grope my way along. Slowly, I would latch on to a few simple words of English, word by word, step by step, until I found I could understand the gist of what at least my teachers were saying, especially if I had studied the lesson in the textbook the night before, translating practically every other word in it into Khmer, which I wrote lightly, in pencil, in the margins.

The words were coming into focus, slowly but surely. But the faces of my classmates at school all still seemed a blur, as if I was seeing them through those thick, bumpy panes of glass that are used in shower stalls.

So I didn't recognize the tall, lanky boy who called

out to me after music class one day. I wasn't even sure he was calling me, because he had mispronounced my name so badly. I glanced back at him, and hesitated. Was he calling me?

Apparently he was. With a few long strides, he had crossed the room and was standing beside me. "Hi, I'm Tom, Nay-kreea," he said awkwardly.

I nodded warily. "My name is Nah-kri," I said. Almost instantly I regretted having corrected his pronunciation. He turned bright red, looking the way I feel when my face burns, mortified. How could I have been so rude?

We both stammered, "Sorry," at the same time, and then we laughed. It was easy to talk after that. As we walked out of class together, Tom said he played the clarinet — and immediately I knew which one he was — the sweet, sensual sounds of the clarinet came from behind me, to the left. He played well.

We talked a bit about the piece we were practicing, and then he said, "I . . . I heard some of your music last night, some Cambodian music. It was nice."

"You sure?" I asked. "Not Thai?" Thai and Cambodian music were similar, and I knew it was much easier to get Thai music cassettes, since they had a thriving music industry and Cambodia didn't.

"No, it was Cambodian," Tom said. "I asked." It turned out he had heard the music coming from the apartment down the hall from where he lived, and he was so intrigued by it that after a while he knocked on their door. "I introduced myself as a neighbor, said welcome to the apartment and stuff. I even brought some chocolate chip cookies on a plate."

I smiled. "They Cambodian?"

"Yes, from Baa-tham-bong," he said, very carefully.

"That was good. You said it right."

"Thanks . . . I try," he said.

We had walked out of school by now, since music was the last period of the day. It was sunny outside, and the snow had almost completely melted, so that tufts of grass were poking through, a tender green.

We walked down the sidewalk together, and the sunshine actually felt warm on my face. It had seemed so unnatural at first, this pale winter sunshine that cast light but no warmth. Tom said the Cambodian family had arrived just two weeks ago, and didn't speak much English yet.

"They have kids?" I asked, my heart beating faster. How wonderful it would be to have a girl my own age to chat and laugh with again!

"Babies. I saw two or three crawling around. And one boy who's going to be in fifth grade."

So young, I thought, disappointed. More Yann's age than mine.

Tom said that if I liked, he could borrow their tape and make a copy of it for me, "in case, you know . . . you miss that kind of music."

I nodded. *"Aw-kun,"* I said. "That means 'Thank-you.'"

Three days later, he caught up with me outside school. "I have the tape," he announced.

He rummaged in his backpack, and produced not just a tape, but a small contraption.

"What's that?" I asked.

"A tape recorder. The tape is in it, all ready to go."

I looked at it in his outstretched hands, but made no move to take it.

"Here, want me to show you how it works? You just have to press this button here . . ." He tried to press the machine into my hands, but I stepped back. He was getting too close, and besides, I didn't know what this meant. Was he trying to sell me the machine? Was he giving it to me? I had heard that in America, if a girl accepted a ring from a boy, it meant she would marry him. What about accepting a tape-playing machine? Did it mean I might have to dance with him? Kiss him? I took another step back — a big step.

"I . . . I don't want it," I stammered.

"But you said . . ."

"Just the tape . . . ," I said. Surely a single tape would be all right to accept.

"Do you have a tape recorder at home?" he asked.

I had to admit that I did not.

"I didn't think so," he said. "So just borrow this one, and give it back to me when you're done."

Still I hesitated.

"Look, it's all right," he said. "I have an extra."

Extra — that I understood. "Extra" was a very American word. Americans seemed to have extras of everything. "You sure?" I asked.

Tom grinned. For answer he pushed the button, and handed the machine over to me.

For a few steps we walked in silence. At first I could hear nothing, just the faint whirring of the machine. Then a few random notes as the musicians tuned up their instruments. I could almost see them, sitting in a semicircle on the floor of the bare stage, off to the side, as the classical dancers performed at center stage.

Dressed in white, their high collars stiff, their buttons a shiny gold, their faces gentle and solemn.

And then the music started — first, the rippling notes from a bamboo xylophone, followed by a quiet, rhythmic drumming, and then the strong, rich cry of the horn. Suddenly, I felt as if Teeda was right there, so close that I had only to reach out to touch her. I shut my eyes, and saw her start the first slow steps of her dancing. The image was so powerful that I felt engulfed in sensation, as if I was standing in the middle of a huge monsoon rainstorm. Except that instead of raindrops beating down, it was memories. I felt overwhelmed.

I opened my eyes, and turned the music off. My heart was beating fast, and I had trouble breathing. Tom was looking at me with concern.

"What's the matter," he asked. "You okay?"

I shook my head. Then I nodded. I didn't trust myself to talk, especially in a foreign language. I just wanted to retreat into the safety of my own room, and calm down.

"I take this," I managed to say, then started running home, my backpack bumping awkwardly behind me, the tape recorder with its precious cassette clutched in my hand.

Back home, and inside my room, with the door not just closed but locked, I looked at the tape recorder. Through the tiny plastic window I could see the tape inside. That's all it is, I told myself. A tape, a long thin ribbon spooled inside a plastic case. And yet somehow it contained a whole world, a world so rich and beautiful, so total, that I could not bear to think of it as having been reduced to this one flimsy tape. I took it out and held it in my hand. It was so light. I thought of playing it quietly, but didn't want my family hearing the music and barging into my room. I wanted the music and the memories all to myself. And so for the rest of the afternoon, I sat there on my mattress, holding the tape, until the twilight faded into dusk, and Ma called me to come out for dinner.

All that weekend, I kept to myself, relieved that my family was too distracted by other concerns to notice that I was spending so much time in my room. With the door closed, I had progressed to putting my ear right up against the tape recorder, and turning on the music very softly. That way, I was able to listen to a few bars of the music. But no more. After the first few minutes, I would have to turn it off, and let the silence and solitude wash over me, soothing me. It was like eating a salty dried plum — you had to lick and nibble tiny bits from it, little by little, because the taste was so intense.

I loved the sound, but it stirred up something so disturbing that I didn't dare get too close to it. So I would lie on my mattress, and listen to a few moments, then shut it off, calm myself down, then after a while, listen to a bit more.

Teeda — if only Teeda were here, I thought, we could play the tape and listen to the music together. And then she would get up and start to dance, and I would slip behind her and follow in her footsteps, lifting my ankle when she did, stretching my arm as she lifted hers. And together we would practice the dance of the apsaras, celestial beings rising from the turmoil of the world into the calm heavens. Step by careful step, we would practice this until we could move in near-perfect unison.

As I thought about this, I started to flex one foot, circling my ankle and moving my toes as Teeda used to do to prepare for dancing. I looked at my bare foot, and marveled at how reassuringly familiar it looked, brown and supple and rough. It seemed like such a long time since I had been aware of my bare feet, after these long winter months having them encased in thick socks and shoes. I felt a sudden impulse to sink my bare feet into mud again, and to squeeze some soil between my toes.

And, in fact, the weather had become warmer with each passing day, and the sunshine lasted a little longer. It felt as if the earth was slowly thawing, as if the sunlight was soaking right into the soil, the way rain soaks into parched earth, stirring new life into everything. Starting from the bottom and leeching upward, first the grass, then the shrubs, then the smaller trees would take on a tender green hue. I had of course been told spring would come, but in the thick of winter, when everything in the world seemed to have shrunken into a cold, dead shadow of itself, it was impossible to imagine how things would come alive again.

So I decided to go outside, and walk around barefoot. There was a small creek running along the far side of our apartment building, with a narrow trail cutting across it to the bus stop on the main road. I had explored that trail enough to know that there was a spot under a willow tree, which I had grown to like. The last time I had been there, the willow leaves hadn't grown in yet, but the branches draped down low, shading a small area from view.

I got dressed in a loose blouse and my sarong, and, flinging Teeda's scarf around me, slipped out of the apartment with the tape recorder.

It was breezy outside, and the sun was high in a cloudless blue sky. I made my way to the spot under the willow tree, and settled comfortably on a flat rock by the riverbank.

The jagged sheet of ice over the stream had melted, and the long strands of willow branches had leafed out, and were waving gently in the breeze. They looked like the tips of a bamboo grove — except upside down. But then of course they'd look upside down, I thought, because aren't we on the other side of the world? I smiled at the silly thought, and made a mental note of telling it to Yann.

I sat down on the rock, and peeled off my socks and shoes. I wriggled my toes. All these months in America, I thought, and they had never touched American soil. Well, today they would, and I would become truly American. I had made it through their long bleak winter; I had learned their difficult language, and I had even made an American friend or two. So today, I decided now, I would celebrate, by playing my Cambodian music, and digging my bare feet into American soil.

Taking a deep breath, I pushed the play button on the tape recorder. This time when the music started, I was ready for it. I listened to it, and let it carry me along with it.

I got up, and felt the cool moist earth under my feet. Slowly, I walked down to the edge of the river and dug my toes into the mud there. The slippery coolness felt so familiar that I gasped. It was as if I was back wading in the stream near the work camp in Phum Thmei, secretly trying to catch fish, or to practice dance steps with Teeda.

A passing breeze rustled the weeping willow branches, and carried the music over to me. There was something in the way the long supple leaves swayed to the music that reminded me of Teeda. Gently, I started swaying to the music too, following the movements of the willow branches just as I used to follow Teeda's. Arching my fingers, I straightened my back and shoulders, and lifted first one flexed foot, then the other.

And so I started dancing again, and Teeda was with me, in me, guiding my movement along step by step as the music played. I felt her close by as we moved together in unison.

At first I was stiff, and my fingers wouldn't turn up

far enough, and I found I had forgotten many of the gestures and the poses. I felt like I couldn't do anything right, not even the simplest things. But slowly, as the music played on, and as the willow branches guided me, it came back, the feel of the dance and the sense of how I should move, and I began to trust my body to move for me, instead of controlling it.

It was all starting to come together again — the way the music fitted the movements, the controlled dignity of the dance, even the way the shadows shifted and the colors played in the dancing light. The world had seemed gray and flat for so long that now I was stunned at the richness of the colors and movement I saw around me.

A strong ray of sunlight caught the sparkles of river water, spotlighting a daffodil rising from the dead leaves. Swaying slightly on its thick stem, it looked a little like the lotus buds that we used when practicing dancing. I reached over and plucked it, liking the way it dipped and nodded as I held it up. Just like the way Teeda's lotus had moved when she danced with it, that last time, at dawn.

I remembered the way she would sometimes look back over her shoulder at me and smile, or how she would say, "That's it, just step into my footsteps," as I would look for the imprint of her bare feet in the mud ahead of me. And guided by those footsteps, I would dance on after her, confident that I was moving exactly as she had moved.

And there, on the cool mud before me, I saw it — the imprint of bare feet. I gasped. She was really there! Teeda was really there, dancing and leaving footsteps for me to follow. For one wildly exhilarating moment, I thought she was really with me again. The moment passed, and I realized that those footsteps had been my own.

Abruptly, I stopped dancing. Why go on? What was I trying to do, playing with memories of dead people?

There, I had to admit it. Teeda was dead.

Teeda was dead, and nothing I could do would bring her back. I could play this music as loud and for as long as I wanted, but I wouldn't see her dance to it again. My sister was gone. She would never dance again, never practice and perform the apsara role to perfection, never breathe life into those classical gestures. Teeda was dead.

The wail started up slow and quiet at first, as I tried to keep it compacted inside of me. But then in an explosion of dark splinters, it surged out, long and shrill. I clamped the scarf over my mouth, tried to clamp down my sobs, to keep it contained, to fight it down, wrest it back down. But there was no containing it — it seeped and surged and spun out, it burst out of me, wild, unleashed, and furious.

I wept, I raged.

Then the music stopped. Not ended, but stopped. Abruptly, in the middle of a bar.

I looked up, and there was my mother, kneeling by the tape recorder on the flat rock. So she must have heard the music, followed it to me, and turned it off. How long she had been there, how much she had seen, I had no idea.

And then she came to me and held me and rocked me. In slow rhythmic silence she rocked me, until the storm of grief had passed and I was limp and drained and empty. She rocked me and I allowed myself to be rocked, and she held me and I allowed myself to be held. She talked to me, and I allowed myself to listen.

Once upon a time, she said, rocking and talking, talking and rocking, a long, long time ago, the gods and the demons were engaged in a terrible tug-of-war, holding onto either end of a gigantic snake and using it to churn up the ocean, creating huge waves of foam between. But out of this awful turmoil, lovely apsaras were created, and they . . .

"I know, I know . . ." I murmured. "Teeda told me."

For a moment my mother was silent. "When?" Ma asked quietly.

"When I was sick," I whispered, my voice shaky. "And then she showed me, by dancing it, just before . . . just before . . ."

"Before she died," Ma nodded. "It's all right, we all die. We're not goddesses; we're not made of stone."

"It's *not* all right," I said. "I want her back. I want to see her dance as an apsara."

"She can," Ma said firmly, "through you. When you dance, Teeda is dancing, too, through you. That's what dance is about, child. Not just the steps and gestures, no matter how beautiful they may be. It's about the spirit in the steps. The apsara goddesses had the courage to dance through the churning waves, from the bottom of the ocean until they reached the open sky. . . . Each of them, these lovely apsaras, had the courage to live with joy. And Teeda did, too. That's why she kept practicing the dance, and that's what she was trying to teach you. Not just how to dance, but how to live fully, with joy.

And you, Nakri, you must keep dancing, and keep alive the joy, too."

And then, so gently that at first I didn't know what she was doing, she took my right hand and smoothed the fingers straight, and bent them backward, gently and then with more pressure, first at the knuckles, then the middle joints, finally the tips, flexing, flexing them backward. She was flexing my fingers back, just as she had done years and years ago, when I was a little girl trying to follow in my big sister's footsteps. She wanted my fingers supple, so that I could start dancing again. And I helped her.

We started that very morning, as the icicles melted into the river water and the geese flew overhead. We played the tape again, and listened quietly to the music, absorbing it as the soil under us absorbed the spring sun. And then we began the long, slow process of dancing again, she to teach, I to learn, and both of us to hold Teeda close to our hearts.

And gradually, not that day nor the day after or even the year after, I began to sometimes feel that effortless sense of sweetness that had infused my childhood. Through the long dark years of living in terror under the

Khmer Rouge, the struggle to escape and then to adapt to a new life, I had almost forgotten that feeling. But with dancing — not always, but sometimes — with the music throbbing in my veins, and my body moving in synchronized rhythm with it — I would feel what Teeda must have felt, what the apsara goddesses themselves might have felt — that even while caught in a stormy sea, they must keep dancing, dance on through the roiling waves so that when they finally surged up toward the open air, their grace and joy would light up the world.

Minfong Ho:
My Parallel Journey

Cambodia. The word conjures up images of mass graves, emaciated refugees, unending warfare. Yet it wasn't always so.

When I was growing up in Thailand in the 1950s and '60s, neighboring Cambodia was a prosperous and fertile country, ruled by a benign young king. It was only a few hours' drive away from where I lived in Bangkok, and although I had never been there, I think my own childhood was probably very similar to a Cambodian child's then. After the monsoon rains, I would wade knee-deep in mud after wiggly catfish; in the marketplaces, I squeeze-tested ripening mangoes and star fruit; sometimes I had to sit still for long hours as saffron-robed Buddhist monks chanted their prayers; and on rare occasions I would watch, awestruck, as glistening classical dancers glided as gracefully as if they really were danc-

191

ing for the gods. The culture and history of Thailand and Cambodia had been intertwined for centuries, and it was reflected in the details of daily life.

But by 1970, when I left Thailand at age eighteen to study in the United States, the differences between Thailand and Cambodia were widening drastically. The Vietnam War had cast its long shadow on the whole region, spilling into Cambodia and embroiling it in a long and bloody civil war, despite King Sihanouk's attempt to walk an uneasy tightrope between the communist Khmer Rouge under Pol Pot, and the pro-American government under Lon Nol.

I followed the news events as best as I could, but I was alone on the other side of the world and often felt very cut off from home. One winter night, I saw a performance of classical Cambodian dance at Cornell University, where I was studying, and afterward, walking across the cold, dark campus, I was engulfed in a strong wave of homesickness, because the music and movements of that dance had evoked my own memories of Thailand so powerfully. I was more determined than ever before to return home as soon as I could.

After all, as a foreign student, I had no intention of staying in America after I graduated. I was not an immigrant; my family and my future were "back home." And so, after four years in the United States, I did return home, first to Singapore, where my parents had moved, and shortly after that back to Thailand, where I took on a teaching job in Chiengmai.

So, for much of the events described in the first half of this book, I was again "next door" to Cambodia. From 1975 to 1979, the communist Khmer Rouge took over Cambodia and the cities were forcibly evacuated, families were broken apart and forced into separate labor camps, and hundreds of thousands more were either executed in mass "killing fields" or died from disease, starvation, or exhaustion.

I was only a few hundred miles away, and yet, all that time, I knew very little of the nightmare that Cambodia had been plunged into. Nobody knew. Cambodia was sealed off from the outside world, with its phone lines cut, its foreign journalists banished, and its borders heavily patrolled and planted with land mines to prevent its people from escaping.

By the time it was over, almost two million Cambodians, out of a population of roughly eight million, had died.

It is hard to grasp the sheer magnitude of that. Think

of the deaths at the destruction of the World Trade Center on September 11th. Now imagine that happening in fifteen different cities across the United States at the same time, every single day for four years in a row. The deaths from that would amount to about a quarter of the American population, roughly the proportion of the Cambodian people who were killed.

It was only in 1979, when the Vietnamese army invaded Cambodia and ousted the Khmer Rouge, that the world began to get a glimpse of what Cambodia had gone through. In the chaos following the invasion, Cambodians by the hundreds of thousands flooded across to the Thai-Cambodian border, desperate for food and medical aid.

Like everyone else, I watched, horrified, at the scenes televised over the news, of the famished refugees, and in 1980 I volunteered to work as a nutritionist with a relief agency on the Thai-Cambodian border.

My first glimpse of the scene at Nong Chan was far worse than anything I could ever have imagined. From a tall bamboo watchtower erected at the middle of one camp, I saw countless thousands of people, like a churning brown ocean, stretched out in every direction on the flat plain, as far as the eye could see. Many of them were wounded and sick, most of them were stick thin, and all of them were uprooted. It was devastating.

But then, as I walked through the sprawling refugee camp, a strange thing happened. I began to feel at home. It was almost like walking around my old neighborhood. Mothers were stirring pots of rice over campfires, boys splashed water from mud puddles onto their buffaloes, and men were hammering at the axles of cart wheels. And the children! The children were everywhere — skinny, ragged, mischievous. They reminded me of myself at that age. I remember watching one group playing with rubber bands and clay marbles, and I thought that if I were just a few years younger, I would have wanted to join in their games. Far from being victims of war, these people — especially the children — were its victors, simply because they had survived against all odds.

The longer I worked on the border, the more I admired the children I was working for. My work was simple enough. I was part of a team that was responsible for buying truckloads of fresh vegetables and charcoal from the Thai markets, getting it cooked at the thatched kitchens in the refugee camps, and making sure that the food was distributed to the thousands of malnourished kids there. There was never time to get to know any of the children individually, but I felt as if I had developed enough of a sense of kinship with them to imagine what their lives might have been like, and what those lucky few who got to settle in America might have felt.

I returned to America at roughly the same time the first wave of Cambodian immigrants arrived there. This time around, I had become an immigrant of sorts myself — an accidental immigrant. I had married an American citizen while in Thailand, a classmate from my Cornell days who had also worked on the Thai-Cambodian border. As his wife, but retaining my original citizenship, I was now classified as a "Permanent Alien," a sort of twilight-zone status that described my state of mind pretty accurately. As a new immigrant, I came to know firsthand what it felt like to be cut off from one's roots, and to have to try to adapt as a transplant on foreign soil.

I could no longer take refuge in my status as a temporary visitor to America. I cared more when I stuck out like a sore thumb and had to try to blend in more. I understood what it was like to try hard to adjust to new surroundings while at the same time trying to retain old loyalties and memories. I struggled with the same question immigrants often do: When changing oneself becomes a means of survival, why does it so often feel like an act of betrayal?

And, like all immigrants, I desperately wanted there to be a bridge between my new life in America and my old life at home. I was luckier than most because there was such a bridge for me, and I could cross from one side of the world to the other and back again, because our work took us to many different countries. The nomadic life wasn't easy, but at least it allowed me to maintain ties with friends and family in both America and Asia, a luxury many Cambodian immigrants would not have.

In the process of these crossings, my husband and I raised one child in the United States, a second one in Singapore and Thailand, and a third in Laos and Switzerland. It was shortly after the third one was born in 1991 that I made one important crossing that I had never done before — into Cambodia.

After a decade of political turmoil, an uneasy truce had been worked out in Cambodia in the early '90s. Many Cambodians who had settled overseas were taking advantage of this new stability to visit their homeland. Because my husband was assigned to a job in

Phnom Penh, I also went there, leaving our three children with my mother in Singapore.

Cambodia was not what I had expected. The familiar was even more familiar than I had anticipated, and the strange even more strange. With a good Cambodian friend by my side, I walked easily around the streets and temples, the marketplaces and villages, and felt as if I was almost back in Thailand. Yet I would also attend memorial services for the dead, hear gunshots in the streets, and walk through museums with piles of human skulls as exhibits, and I knew that I was in Cambodia. My friend good-humoredly introduced me to her wide circle of family and friends, and through her I talked to monks and peddlers, schoolteachers and soldiers, bureaucrats and beggars. Everyone had a story, and every story was compelling. Always, there was an intense undercurrent of both sadness and of hope in their stories that was distinctively Cambodian.

In the decade or so since that visit, I have watched from afar as Cambodia lurched its way toward a semblance of peace. In 1993, under U.N. supervision, national elections were successfully held, with an incredible 4.2 of 4.7 million registered voters turning out. Another coalition government was formed on the basis of that election. The refugee camps on the Thai border were dismantled, and the 350,000 Cambodians sent home. The Khmer Rouge continued to weaken until, with Pol Pot's death in 1998, it was no longer a threat to anyone. In 1998, elections were held again, and despite much infighting, yet another coalition government has been set up and maintained. Cambodia is still one of the poorest countries in the world, and corruption and human rights violations are still facts of life there, but at least there has been a growing sense of stability. The future of Cambodia remains uncertain, but I think back to what I saw and felt during my visit there, and one particular image stays with me.

It is of a man on a bicycle, riding through the potholed streets of Phnom Penh at dawn. In one hand he is holding aloft a huge bouquet of helium balloons, the bright reds and blues bobbing against the drab gray of the buildings. As he rides along he's calling out his wares, and children tumble out from doorways and side streets, laughing and chasing after his balloons. As I watched him that morning, I felt sure that Cambodia would make it through even this very darkest chapter of its history.

Acknowledgments

Classical dance has always been an integral part of Khmer culture, as deeply engraved in the hearts of the Cambodian people as it is in the stone carvings of their ancient temple at Angkor Wat. This treasured legacy was almost annihilated during the mass destruction and genocide by the Khmer Rouge regime between 1975 and 1979. Since 1980, however, the surviving dancers in Cambodia have struggled to preserve and revive Khmer dance, while teaching a new generation of artists and musicians. Part of the royalties from this book will be donated to the Fund for Cambodian Culture (http://www.nefa.org/projinit/cambart/camb_donate.html) to help support programs at the Royal University of Fine Arts in Phnom Penh, which focus on the preservation and transmission of traditional Khmer dance, music, and theater.

I am very grateful to Hannah Phan, who shared with me many of her experiences as a child in Phnom Penh, and a teenager in a work camp during the Khmer Rouge years. She read each draft of the manuscript carefully, and provided me with many insightful suggestions. Similarly, my friendships with Sophan Ros, Kem Sos, and Sina Than helped me understand and appreciate the many nuanced differences between Cambodia and Thailand. Sopeap Than, who hosted my stay in Phnom Penh, was especially wonderful as a guide and interpreter during my visits to various sites and villages in the area.

My old friend Ben Kiernan graciously consented to read this simple story, providing several useful comments along the way, as did Jay Hart and Chiranan Prasertkul. And I am particularly grateful to my husband, John Dennis, whose own work with the refugees on the Thai-Cambodian border led me to work there as well, and to eventually develop the strong respect and admiration I have for the people and culture of Cambodia.